BETRAYAL OF MAGIC

BETRAYAL OF MAGIC

THE SARIAH CHRONICLES™ BOOK TWO

PETER GLENN

MICHAEL ANDERLE

DISRUPTIVE IMAGINATION

Copyright © 2020 LMBPN Publishing
Cover by Mihaela Voicu http://www.mihaelavoicu.com/
Cover copyright © LMBPN Publishing
A Michael Anderle Production

LMBPN Publishing
PMB 196, 2540 South Maryland Pkwy
Las Vegas, NV 89109

Version 1.01, July 2020
ebook ISBN: 978-1-64971-063-5
Print ISBN: 978-1-64971-064-2

THE BETRAYAL OF MAGIC TEAM

Thanks to our Beta Readers
Larry Omans, Kelly O'Donnell, Jim Caplan

Thanks to our JIT Readers

Veronica Stephan-Miller
Dorothy Lloyd
Diane L. Smith
Angel LaVey

Editor

SkyHunter Editing Team

CHAPTER ONE

"So Gabe, I was thinking," Sariah started. She took a step toward him and beamed at him with eyes that were glowing like diamonds.

Gabriel let out a massive sigh. "I know what you're going to ask, Sariah. The answer is no."

"Aw, come on," she whined. "You know you want to."

Gabe gave her a sideways glance and shrugged. "You're right, I do. Or at least I did once. But it's still a no."

"Humph!" She turned her back to him. She thought about walking out of their little shared room in The Dragonfly for good measure, but where would she go?

Despite the fact she'd spent the better part of the last month in and near the city of Stratton, she didn't know the area very well. Apart from her occasional trips to Market Square and her bout with Lucien, she'd stuck to the little inn.

It wasn't that she didn't like an adventure. She just felt lost in the vastness of open spaces. She'd grown up in a small mining town. Big open areas weren't really her thing. She was much more comfortable in close quarters.

She bit her lip. Trying to get Gabriel to do anything was like pulling teeth. He was completely impossible, especially lately.

"Please?" she implored. "I'll do whatever you say, I swear. I'll be the perfect student."

Gabe let out another deep sigh. It was like it was his signature move. Normally it annoyed her, but today she let it slide.

"I-" he started. "I just don't know if it's…" He paused for a moment and threw his hands in the air. "Bah!" he added. Then he stopped speaking entirely.

Sariah frowned and turned her head to see if he was looking at her. He wasn't. She felt disappointed and deflated.

Then she mentally kicked herself. Why do I care whether or not he looks at me anyway? she thought. Ugh.

Somehow Gabe always seemed to know what buttons to press. The two of them were like oil and water - they just didn't mix well. Not that she wanted them to.

Sariah tugged on Gabe's shoulder. "Come on," she purred. "You know you want to train me in physical magic-y stuff. You've been asking to do it for so long now. Why the sudden change of heart?"

She hoped appealing to his egotistical side would work better.

Gabe turned around to face her fully. There was a look of weariness in his eyes. In fairness, the last week and a half had been rough on him. He'd nearly died out in the woods while she'd gone off chasing Lucien.

He'd managed to heal himself, and the rest of them as well once Sariah had finally relented and let him use his magic powers on her. She'd felt a little icky about it at the time, but in the end, it hadn't felt bad.

The only problem was Gabe had been grumpy and sullen ever since, almost like she'd wounded his ego or something.

Men could be so hard to understand sometimes.

"It's just, I just don't know if it's a good idea anymore," Gabe admitted at last.

"Not a good idea?" She felt her cheeks start to grow hot as her temper flared. "What is that supposed to mean?"

Gabe lifted a finger and pointed it in her direction then opened his mouth, but no words came out. A second later he dropped the finger and lowered his head onto his chest.

Sariah rolled her eyes at him. "Ugh, not this again. You know I hate the silent treatment."

Gabe laughed, completely spoiling his sullen, withdrawn look. "I wasn't giving you the silent treatment. I don't even know what to say, sometimes, you know?"

"Uh, no. No, I don't." She shook her head while she spoke. "Never had that problem."

He snorted. "Yeah, I've noticed."

Sariah put her hands on her hips and gave him a defiant stare. She thought about throwing a pillow at his stupid head, but that hadn't done her any good the last time. Gabe was surprisingly agile.

Gabe held up his hands in self-defense. "Easy now. You know I didn't mean it like that." He pulled on his face. "This is getting us nowhere. Let's start this conversation over."

"What, so you can tell me no all over again?" she crossed her arms and stuck up her nose. "No thank you. I can get that from Harvey."

Gabe groaned. "I give up. There's just no winning with you, is there?"

She cocked her head to the side and smiled. "There is if you give me what I want." She gave him a flirty wink.

Gabe sighed again and turned away from her, so she crept up behind him and put one hand gently on his shoulder.

"Hey," she said softly. "Is this about your special little stones? I'll be gentle this time, I promise."

Sariah was referring to the training stones Gabe had used during their first magic lesson. She'd been a little less than careful with one of them and it had developed a large crack. Gabe had claimed he was over the incident, but every now and then he'd bring it up, so she knew that wasn't the case.

He gave her a look that was part shock and part frustration. He laughed and shook his head. "No. No, it's not about the stones."

"Are you sure? I'll buy you a new one if you want. Don't know where I'd get one, but I'm sure I could find another one of those stupid rocks somewhere in a town this size."

He lifted up a hand to try and silence her. "You just don't get it, do you?"

Sariah wrinkled her nose. "It's kinda hard, seeing as you won't even tell me what 'it' is."

Once more, Gabe sighed. "You're impossible sometimes."

Sariah smiled up at him. "Not when I get what I want. Come on. It can't be that bad, can it?"

He turned to face her and moved in closer until they were only inches apart. She could feel the heat of his breath on her cheeks and it made them tingle a little bit. It was strangely arousing being close to him like this. She liked it, though at the same time it made her feel uncomfortable.

He slowly raised one finger and put it on her chin, lifting her face until their eyes were locked, which only increased the tension.

Sariah was so focused on him she figured a lightning bolt could break through the windows and she wouldn't even notice.

Briefly, she wondered what he was thinking. Was he planning to kiss her? And if so, would she want it? Heat rose to her cheeks and she had to admit part of her would say yes.

Gabe leaned his head in until his lips were practically brushing up against her ear. The closeness felt even more invigorating. In a hushed tone he whispered to her, "It's still a no."

Sariah shoved him hard enough to send him flailing backward. The moment was gone, replaced by frustration.

"Grr!" she scowled. She turned her back to him again.

She glanced over her shoulder for a half-second and Gabe was sitting looking sheepish, so she looked away again before he could notice her.

"I could find someone else you know!" she shouted over her shoulder.

Gabe scoffed. "And just who would you find, anyway?"

"Maybe I'll track down your old mentor, Jakob. I bet he'd train me." She had no idea how to find him and wasn't about to start looking, but he was the only other person who came to mind. She just hoped it would do the trick.

"Pfft. You'd never find him even if you tried."

Sariah let out a deep breath. He'd called her bluff. So much for that angle. She turned to face him again. "Oh come on! It'll be different this time, I swear! I just know I can get the hang of it this time!"

Gabe rubbed his chin for a second. "I'm just not sure. Are you sure you really want it?" He took a step toward her and put a hand on her shoulder. "I mean, I can understand why someone in your position might not. Magic hasn't been the kindest to you. That's probably why it didn't work the last time."

She was taken aback. Had that been his issue this whole time? She grimaced and turned away again so she could think clearly.

In her mind's eye, she went back to the failed magic training session a week prior. Gabe had finally agreed to train her in physical magic, and she had been downright giddy. Only, it hadn't gone so well. She'd tried her best, but after several hours of nothing Gabe had gotten flustered and called the whole thing off.

Am I holding back? she wondered. Is that why I failed last time?

Sariah thought about it earnestly. Magic had done some pretty awful things. It had cost her father his legs and later his life, it had burned down her house, and so much more. But it had also saved her and allowed her to rescue Harvey when he was in trouble. Magic was just a tool, and it was the person behind it who chose to wield it for good or ill.

Perhaps her latent dislike for magic had held her back, but she could get past it. She could make it work for her. She had to. It was the only way she could protect her friends from people like the Master.

And Bear, of course. She couldn't forget about her favorite dog. She and the mangy mutt had grown quite close of late.

"Yes. I'm positive." She faced him and gave him a firm nod. "I want you to train me further in the magic-y arts. Physical magic, nature magic. Everything. Teach me all of it."

Gabe pulled on his face again. "Hmm," he started. "I like the enthusiasm, but I still don't know."

"What could I do to convince you?" She went over to him and pulled on his shirt. "I'll do anything."

"Anything, eh?" He rubbed his chin and gave her a sideways glance. "I could be convinced."

Sariah shoved him again. "Ugh, you men! You're all the same." She put her hands on her hips. "You know what I meant."

Gabe let out a slight chuckle. "Okay, okay. Sorry." His face sobered. "But what if?"

Sariah shook her head vigorously. "It won't happen. I swear it. Cross my heart and hope to die. I'm committed. I can do this." She made the symbol of a cross over her chest.

Gabe raised one of his eyebrows. "And if you do fail again?"

"Then I'll never bring it up ever again. I pinky swear."

She held out her pinky in front of her. "You know there's no breaking a pinky swear."

Gabe looked at the offered pinky and let out a hearty laugh, then took it in his own. "You know I could never say no to you. Fine. We'll do it tonight after everyone has gone to bed."

Sariah let the fact he'd spent the last week telling her no about a thousand times slide. It wasn't important now.

"Yay!" she squealed.

Happy at last, she practically ran out of the room. At the last moment, she turned to Gabe and called out, "Oh, and I'm bringing Harvey along, too. See you tonight!"

It was only fair. Harvey had been begging to learn magic ever since they'd gotten back to the inn. He deserved a shot, too.

Gabe's jaw dropped halfway to the floor. "Harvey!" he scowled. "I never said anything about training two people! Hey, wait!"

He yelled out a few other things, but Sariah was already halfway down the hallway and she couldn't understand any of them.

With a big grin on her face, she headed downstairs to talk to Evelyn, their innkeeper. There were good smells coming from the main room. It was lunchtime and she was going to need lots of energy for the night to come.

The man known only as the Master knelt on the ground. At his feet lay the broken, bleeding body of a magical assassin once known as Lucien.

He placed one finger into the pool of blood seeping out of the assassin's body and stared at it in wonder for a moment. Then he rubbed the blood between two of his fingers and sniffed it.

"It's a pity, Daniel," the Master said.

The hooded figure behind him nodded. "Yes, Master, it is."

The Master stood straight. Today he had taken on the appearance of a tall warlord, easily six and a half feet tall with a mohawk and various markings painted under his eyes. Half of his entire body was covered in similar markings, and the other half was covered in furs.

He flexed his currently broad shoulders and appreciated how powerful it made him feel, even if it was all fake. He'd pick a new appearance tomorrow. He never used the same appearance twice if he could avoid it.

No, the true power lay coagulating in a puddle on the ground, wasted. Lucien's blood. Everyone's blood, actually, where the nanocytes that powered magic lay, and he was close to unlocking more of their secrets.

The Master rubbed his chin with the fingers coated in blood. "Do you know why it's a pity, my dear Daniel?" he asked his assistant.

His assistant looked down at the broken body for a moment, then back up. He furrowed his brow. "Because Lucien failed in his mission, sir?"

The Master let out a deep, hearty laugh. His whole chest shook in the process. It was a good feeling. He needed to laugh more often. Life couldn't all be about ruling his criminal empire.

"That is, indeed, a pity, my dear Daniel." He shook his

head and patted his assistant on the shoulder. "But no, that's not why it's a true pity. The true pity is he died. Had he but lived, at least he would have been of some use to me as a test subject."

His thoughts turned back to his experiments. He had a test subject waiting for him back in his lab right now, actually, but this took precedence. His little guest would have to wait.

Daniel nodded. "Of course, Master, I understand."

"I thought you might." The Master gave Daniel a hearty slap on his shoulder, then his gaze returned to the broken corpse at his feet. "And yet I wonder…"

Daniel cocked his head to the side. "Wonder what, Master?"

"Bah!" The Master waved off Daniel's curiosity dismissively with one of his massive hands. How he hated that trait in a subordinate. It could cause so many problems for so many people.

Still, he supposed Daniel had earned the right to be curious this one time. The man was quite the faithful helper, and it was the Master's own fault for uttering his musings out loud in front of him.

A long, slow breath escaped his lips. "No, that's a fair question," he admitted. "The situation here, it makes me wonder if my focus has been in the wrong place." His thoughts went again to his experiments, but he shook his head to clear it and return his attention to the present.

"Lucien was one of my best assassins. A top general as well," the Master continued. "And yet here he is, lying dead at my feet."

Daniel nodded once but said nothing.

"To top it off, he wasn't brought down by an army of rebels, but by a single little girl."

"It is curious, Master."

The Master nodded. "It is curious indeed. It makes me wonder, have I been so wrapped in my experiments lately I've grown partially blind to the developing world around me?" He rubbed his chin again. "What could have given one tiny little girl the power to topple one of my most promising students of the last few years?"

His assistant took a couple of steps closer. "What should we do about it, Master?"

The Master looked him in the eye and shrugged. "Maybe it's time for a change in plans." He lowered his head for a moment, lost in thought, then raised it again. "Put calls into my generals in the field. We will have a council three weeks from today."

Daniel bowed deeply in front of him. "Of course, Master. Your will be done."

"Thank you, Daniel." He gave his assistant a slight smile. "You have always served me so unfailingly."

Daniel bowed again and started to back away, then stopped and furrowed his brow. "Master?" he called out.

The Master's ears perked up and he turned his head halfway toward the man. "Yes, dearie? What else is there to discuss?" He growled slightly, annoyed at the interruption.

"What would you have me do with the body?" Daniel asked, pointing to Lucien's twisted remains.

The Master scowled. He gave Lucien's dead body a single swift kick to the midsection. The force was enough to make the body turn over so Lucien's dead, foggy eyes faced upward toward the sun.

"Leave it," he ordered. He spat upon Lucien's corpse once for good measure. "Let the animals have their way with what's left of him. Surely they've earned the privilege."

His assistant had a concerned look on his face. "You're not worried someone will find his body?"

The Master scoffed. "And even if they did?" He shook his head. "It's not like it would do them any good. Lucien was an invisible assassin. No one knew who he was. A fact that will serve him well enough in death, I suppose."

He let out another hearty laugh. Once more, laughter lifted his spirits. "Besides, even if someone happened upon his remains, our base of operations is too well hidden. It will remain quite safe, I assure you."

Daniel bowed again. "Of course, Master. You know best."

The Master grinned back at him. The grin went from ear to ear. "Yes, my dear Daniel. Yes, I do."

CHAPTER TWO

Padron made his way to the mines in Chatwick. He was determined to figure out what on Irth could have been so important down there it would have caused all this turmoil. His friend Sariah's life was in chaos, and fer what? A worthless medallion at the bottom of some mineshaft in a hopeless town in the middle of the Alpenwood.

He shook his head. No, that didn't make no sense. People don't kill and destroy fer nothing. There had ta be a reason. Something else was going on in this town, and he had every intention of getting to the bottom of it, and that meant going back into the mines.

The rearick pushed on his mine cart and headed for the entrance to the shaft. The cart held his battle-ax and a handful of low-grade explosives, covered by a couple of blankets and some pickaxes. The hefty weapon would help him get past any human guards who might block his path, and the explosives should take care of anything more stationary.

On his left, the mine foreman sat in a watchtower,

inspecting all of the miners as they came into work. Most were waved through without incident, though the occasional man would be stopped and frisked by a nearby guard.

"Bah," Padron grumbled. "Some lousy policy this is," he added under his breath.

Supposedly, it was for their safety, but that word and the way the foreman wielded it like a deadly weapon to do whatever he pleased made Padron feel sick to his stomach and bile rise into the back of his throat, which he managed to gulp back down.

The line stopped as someone two places in front of him was flagged down and pulled off to the side. Padron shook his head slightly from side to side. Looked like the poor soul was in for one of those intensive searches. He shuddered to think of what that would even mean.

A few more feet forward and he'd be cleared to go into the mines.

He wiped a small bead of sweat off his brow. He was more nervous than he thought.

The person in front of him was waved on through without incident. Now it was his turn to follow. He gave his cart a hefty push forward. As he walked, the mine foreman stared at him and the two of them locked eyes for just a moment. The look the foreman gave him sent a chill down his spine.

Padron smiled and gave the foreman a quick wave of the hand, then set his eyes out in front and went back to pushing his cart.

"Hold," a voice came from his side. It was the foreman. He was coming down from his little tower.

The hair on Padron's neck stood on end. Blast it all, he thought. Was his cover blown already?

The foreman approached slowly. He cocked his head to the side and smiled. "Padron?" the man said in a gentle tone. "I didn't expect to see you back to work so soon."

Padron gave him a weak smile and made a broad sweeping motion with his hands. "Oh well, ya know how it goes, Jeffrey," he answered. "Even a man like me needs money ta eat." He patted his belly a few times for good measure.

Jeffrey chuckled and clapped him on the back. The motion was a little too sudden and Padron almost fell forward. He used the cart to steady himself and keep from falling. "Ain't that the truth," Jeffry replied.

The rearick nodded. "Aye, now if ye will let me, I'd like ta get on with me day."

"Of course." The foreman waved to a nearby guard. "Just have to inspect the cart first. Regulation and all."

"Of course," Padron answered with a weak smile. Inside, his mind was reeling as he tried to think of a way out of his current predicament.

One of the guards came over and glanced inside the cart. He picked up a pickaxe and shuffled the blanket around slightly, then set the tool back down and nodded to the foreman.

"All good," the guard said.

Phew. Thank tha Patriarch he didn't check no further.

Jeffrey beamed at him. In the sunlight, his smile looked fake. Padron began to wonder if he was going to leave this checkpoint alive. He felt another bead of sweat form at his brow and wanted to wipe it away but was afraid it would look suspicious, so he let it dangle.

"Well wouldn't expect any less from our Padron, now would we?" Jeffrey offered at last.

Padron smiled at him again and chuckled. "Ya know me all too well, Jeffrey."

The foreman waved him onward. Padron pushed the cart forward with a great heave and got out of their gazes as quickly as he could.

Once he was safely within the shadows of the mineshaft, he stopped for a moment and took in a deep breath to steady himself. He'd managed to get past the gate guards without anyone suspecting a thing. That was the easy part. The hard part came next.

He wiped the sweat from his brow with one of his massive hands and headed for the elevator to take him and his goods down to the bottom of the mine.

It didn't take long before he was deep within the bowels of Irth once more. Fortunately, there was no one down on this level today he could see.

The rearick breathed a sigh of relief. Maybe he'd get lucky. Maybe he'd be able to pull off his little mission without running into anyone and return to the surface safe and sound.

Smiling, Padron pushed the minecart off the elevator and made his way forward, quietly whistling an old tune all the while. He dared not make too much noise lest anyone noticed, but he couldn't help but whistle a little.

His smile quickly faded as he rounded a bend and almost smashed head-first into a guard. He darted backward quickly, hoping the guard hadn't seen him.

They have a guard posted all the way down here, too? he thought incredulously.

There was no doubting it now. They were hiding something down here for sure. It was one thing to board off a tunnel because of bad juju, but you didn't post a guard there, too.

Padron took a few deep breaths to steady himself and waited for the guard in the hallway to make a move, but nothing happened. He waited for a count of ten, but still the guard didn't come. He let out a sigh. It appeared he was safe for the moment.

There was still time to formulate a plan for getting past the guy without any fuss. He just had to think of something.

Rummaging around in the cart, he tried to come up with something original but kept going back to his ax. He shrugged his broad shoulders. Ain't nothin' to it, I suppose, he thought. He picked up the weapon and strode forward into the mineshaft with a broad grin on his face.

The guard in the tunnel saw him coming and stood up straighter. "Sorry, sir. No one's allowed down here. Foreman's orders."

Padron smiled at him. "Oh, I'm sorry, sonny. I dinnae know that."

"Sorry again. Now if you'll just be on your way." He made a shooing motion toward the rearick, but Padron kept walking forward anyway.

Padron caught a hint of fear in the guard's eyes as he kept heading straight for him.

"I'm sorry, sir, but please go," the guard insisted. He grabbed onto the sword he was holding just a little tighter.

"I'm sorry, too, lad," Padron said.

When the first blow from the guard came, Padron almost wasn't ready for it. The guard made a high sweeping motion and he had to duck backward to get out of the way.

"Blast it all!" he grunted. He swung his ax at the guardsman as hard as he could, but with the cramped hallway, he wasn't able to get a lot of power behind it and the guard parried easily.

Padron eyed the guard. He had a wicked smile on his face, and he was looking more at his weapon than him.

Another swipe came then, this one a bit lower. The rearick brought his own weapon up to parry the blow with ease, then swung his weapon in a vertical motion to try to get past his opponent's guard.

The guard blocked the blow, but he was forced back into the wall.

Padron smiled, but he didn't have long to enjoy the moment. The guard came at him with a fury of desperate blows, each one short and quick. This forced Padron back into the hallway and allowed the guard to regain his position.

He felt something wet on his arm and looked down to see a fresh cut on his left arm. He hadn't been as good at blocking that onslaught as he'd thought.

Pain shot up his arm, but Padron pushed it aside and redoubled his offensive. He made a wild slash with his ax at his opponent's sword arm.

The guard brought his weapon up to defend against it, but this time the blade shattered against the might of Padron's attack.

A squeal of fear erupted from the guard as he realized what that meant.

Padron made another wild slash and scored a cut on the guard across his midsection. The guard muttered something he couldn't make out, then clutched his stomach and fell to the ground.

He swung his ax once more, severing the guard's head from his body so he couldn't let out a scream to warn any others who might be waiting, then the battle was over.

The rearick slunk up against the nearby wall and checked his arm again. The fresh wound was slick with blood, so he wiped at it with cloth from his shirt. Once the blood had been wiped away and he could see the wound clearly, he could tell it was little more than superficial.

Padron breathed a sigh of relief and wiped the sweat off his brow. Thank tha Patriarch it ain't more serious.

He made his way back to the cart and tore a piece of cloth off the blanket and used it to wrap his wound. The blanket wasn't sterile, but it wasn't overly stained, either so it should do the trick, at least in the short term.

He went back to the guard's body and shoved it out of the way, then took in his next obstacle.

Before him stood a barrier made of solid wood that blocked the passage forward. He tapped on it in a few places. The construction looked hasty but was made of decent quality materials. He might end up needing those explosives, after all.

He spared another glance at the dead guard. Surely, someone would miss him. It wouldn't be hard for a person to put two and two together. It was Padron's first trip back into the mine in weeks, and the guard magically ended up dead. That didn't bode well for him.

Padron shrugged. There was no use worrying about it now. The deed was done. He'd figure out how to deal with it later.

Returning his attention to the wall, he hefted his ax in his hands and smiled. "I'll have ya down in a jiffy," he told the inanimate structure. "Don't ya worry much. This'll only hurt a wee bit."

He hefted his arms back and came down with a massive strike at the barrier. He could feel the wood start to give way almost immediately as his blade hit. A few swings later, and he'd made a decent hole in the wood.

Padron smiled, thankful the explosives would not be necessary. They would have made an awful racket and sent someone after him right away.

The rearick took out a lantern and swung it into the opening he'd made like he was warding off evil spirits. For all he knew, he was but nothing answered him. The corridor beyond the wall was just as empty as it was on his side. More so, even, as his side had a dead body in it.

He cracked his neck and stretched out his shoulders, then got to work. There was quite a bit of barrier to go yet before even someone of his diminutive size could squeeze through.

About ten minutes of swinging later, he'd made himself an entrance. He had to duck to fit, but it was big enough, and he'd spent enough time making the hole as it was. He wasn't sure how long it would be until someone came to relieve the guard, and he didn't want to be here when that happened.

Once he was on the other side, he swung his lantern around in a wide arc. It lit up the walls of the corridor beyond but didn't glint off anything in particular.

Padron took in his surroundings. The small crevasse Sariah had described was not far in front of him, only it didn't look nearly as tight as the girl had described it. He crept forward slowly to inspect it, half-expecting something to jump out and get him, but nothing did. The area was well and truly deserted.

He started his way through the cramped corridor, noting it seemed to be broad enough for him to make it through without too much fuss. It was a tight fit, but Sariah would have had no problem with a corridor of this size. What had the girl been complaining about?

Then he noticed the tool markings, even in the low light. Someone had been through here recently, and they'd used pickaxes to widen the gap. There was no mistaking it. His suspicions were confirmed. They were hiding something down here. Now he just had to figure out what it was.

With his teeth partially clenched in anticipation of another fight, he pushed forward, heading deeper into the corridor.

Before long, the space opened up. He looked around at the walls and was amazed. There were strange markings all over. They didn't look like tool markings, but they didn't look very natural, either. This was it. This must be the mysterious room Sariah had spoken of in those fateful days after the attack.

Going slowly so as not to miss anything, he inspected the walls carefully. He didn't know what he was looking for exactly, only he was pretty sure he'd know it when he saw it.

It didn't take him very long to find something out of the ordinary. Anyone else would have gone right past and dismissed it like it was nothing, but not Padron. With his specific history, he knew better. Embedded in the walls of the room were a bunch of tiny white-colored gems. They didn't look like much to the untrained eye, but Padron had a hunch as to what they might be and what they would mean.

The wheels in his head turned quickly as the pieces started to fall into place. If he was right about the gems, then it would all make sense - the secrecy, the cover-up, the attacks - all of it.

But I have ta be sure.

Working quickly and with deft hands, he used the tip of his pickaxe to work a couple of the gemstones free. He wouldn't need to take many of them to confirm his suspicions. Just a few would suffice.

He didn't want more than that, anyway. If he was right and these gems meant what he thought they did, he wanted as little to do with them as possible.

A moment later, he had what he needed. He placed the glinting stones into one of the pockets of his pants and made his way back out of the corridor, walking fast.

He wasn't sure how long he'd spent in there, but he knew it had been long enough someone could have stumbled across the opening, or the downed guard, quite easily in his absence. He had to get out now and get to safety.

The Matriarch and Patriarch must have been smiling

on him though, for when he came back to the entrance, he found it just as devoid of life as he'd left it.

Padron took a deep breath and went back to his minecart. He pushed it and headed back toward the elevator, humming an old tune and acting like nothing out of the ordinary had happened. It wasn't much longer before he'd get out to freedom.

His trip up the elevator was equally uneventful, but he knew someone would find the mess he'd left behind soon enough.

Once he reached the surface level, he heard the sound of boots crunching against the dirt and some sort of conversation. He couldn't quite make out what they were saying.

Padron's mind raced. Had he been found out already? There was really no way to know. He decided to duck behind the mine cart and hope no one noticed him.

"Can you believe old Jim?" one of the guards was saying as they got closer.

"Pfft. Probably fell asleep again. That poor sop is always noddin' off," another guard said.

Padron's blood froze. They were talking about the guard he'd killed. He just knew it. He stood still, unsure of what to do. He could probably take the guards, but then what? There was no way he could take on all the guards at the mine, nor did he want to.

He decided to wait it out. Sweat poured over his brow anew as he sat there, cramped behind the cart, and waited for the sounds of boots on dirt to diminish. Within a few moments, the noise was gone.

Padron mopped his forehead with his shirt, then made

a beeline for the mine entrance. He had precious little time to make it out now before someone came running back up the mine shaft.

Once he reached the entrance, he spotted the foreman, Jeffrey, sitting on his little perch and acting like nothing had gone on a thousand feet below him.

He tried to pay the man no heed and looked straight forward as he pushed his cart, trying not to act suspicious.

"Wait!" Jeffrey cried. Padron froze. He knew the man was talking to him. "Heading back home so soon?"

Padron turned slowly. He shrugged once, then smiled. "Oh, ye know how tired these old bones can get," he replied with a forced grin. As if to emphasize the point, he rubbed his back a few times and groaned. "I have ta get some rest, methinks." He hoped it would be enough to ward off suspicion.

Jeffrey laughed and waved him onward. "You go rest those weary bones of yours, then. But don't expect to get paid for half a days' work."

Padron chuckled. "Course not, sir." He gave the man a salute for good measure.

Once he was well past the mine, he abandoned the mine cart and took a few deep breaths to calm himself. He had gotten away with his deception, but not for too much longer.

His mind went back to the gemstones jingling around in his pocket. He needed answers about the stones, and there was only one place he could think of to get them. Unfortunately, it wasn't close by. He'd have to make quite the voyage over the mountains to his old hometown to be certain.

The rearick checked behind him, certain guards would rush him any moment, but none came.

Maybe this trip would be a good thing, he thought. It would give time for the current situation in Chatwick to die down, and he liked being off on his own, anyway. He'd be gone for at least a month. Likely even longer. He might even miss Sariah coming home if she ever did.

A big sigh escaped his lips. He would just have to take the risk. If not, then who knew what kind of place Sariah might come back to. Besides, she deserved answers. They all did.

I suppose I could use a vacation after all.

The man known as Jeffrey smiled as he watched Padron disappear into town. Behind him, one of his lackeys was mumbling something incoherent.

"What was that lazybones?" he asked the lackey.

The lackey stood up as straight as he could and saluted. His cheeks were starting to turn red. "Sir, there's been a disturbance in the mine. One of the guards is dead."

Jeffrey rubbed his face, then looked at the lackey. "The one guarding the boarded passageway, I take it?"

"Yes, sir."

He shook his head. "Well, that's disturbing news."

"Sir, has anyone left the mine recently?"

Jeffrey rubbed his chin thoughtfully for a moment. He took a furtive glance in Padron's direction.

"No, no one's left the mine," he lied.

The lackey saluted him again. "We'll scour the mine, sir."

He saluted the man back. "Good. Let me know what you find. Bring me any shred of evidence immediately. I want the perpetrator found and hanged in the town square as an example to others."

The lackey gave him a nod and scurried about his way.

Jeffrey looked in Padron's direction once more. *What game are you playing, old man?*

CHAPTER THREE

Sariah walked through the dimly lit hallway of The Dragonfly with Harvey in tow. It was well after dinner time and
all of the other inn patrons were in their rooms. The two
of them were the only ones moving around.

Time for magic training hour, she thought. The whole
scene reminded her of her first lesson. Gabe had insisted
on a night setting then, too, claiming the secrecy would be
for the best.

In a big city like Stratton, using magic could get you
mistaken for a Dusk Raven, and the last thing she wanted
anyone to do was mistake her for one of them.

Sariah shuddered as she thought about the Dusk
Ravens. It was a common reaction, so common it didn't
even faze her. The Dusk Ravens had been responsible for
her parents' deaths, as she'd learned recently, along with a
kidnapping attempt on Harvey, and were generally all
around considered to be bad people.

She always figured this skulking about and making a

bunch of noise after dark was more suspicious than doing it during daylight hours, but it was hard to convince Gabe.

Her stomach churned as she sauntered up to Gabe's door. Was she really ready this time?

I have to be ready this time. She spared a glance at Harvey. His face wore one of his typical dopey grins and the sight warmed her. Yes, she could do it. For Harvey, if not for herself. If only it still didn't feel so icky.

She let out a sigh and looked resolutely at Gabe's door. The time for doubting herself was over.

I've got this, she repeated in her head several times. It helped a little.

Harvey reached forward and rapped on Gabe's door loud enough to wake half the hallway. The sound jarred Sariah out of her current malaise. She winced and gave him a wry look. "Seriously? We're supposed to be secretive about this, remember?"

Harvey gave her a wounded look. "Sorry," he whispered.

A moment later, the door opened, and Gabe ushered the two of them into the room. After they'd made their way in, Gabe stuck his head out the door and peered around in the dark hallway before sticking his head back in the room and finally shutting and locking the door.

Sariah took in her surroundings. All of the furniture in the room had been pushed to the sides of the room, leaving a big space open in the middle. There was a rug on the floor, but otherwise the center of the room was completely empty. Over in a corner by one of the beds lay Bear, who was snoozing away.

Sariah grinned at the sight of Bear. She'd really come to

love the furry animal in their journey so far. He was a true friend and companion. She went over and scratched him behind the ears.

The beast gave off a contented snort and went back to sleep. She gave him a few more pets for good measure, then stood up and went to stand next to Harvey.

"Good evening," Gabe called out to his two students. "I trust you're both ready?"

Harvey nodded and gave a "Yes, sir!" Sariah gave him a firm nod.

Gabe sighed and rubbed his chin. "Hmm," he muttered. He walked up to both of them until he was in their faces. "Not exactly the enthusiasm I was hoping for. This 'magic-y business' isn't for the faint of heart, you know. You have to really want it."

Sariah reared back a half step. "Hey!" she shot back. "I nodded, didn't I?" She placed her hands on her hips. "Surely, I deserve credit for that, at least."

Gabe threw up his hands in self-defense. "True, true," he admitted slowly. "Still, I expected more." His eyes slowly trailed in Harvey's direction. "From both of you. I'm none too impressed by your attitude, either."

Harvey's eyes grew as wide as saucers. "Who, m-me?" he stammered. "I'm ready for this. I've wanted this for a month now."

Their teacher's eyes went to Sariah and he looked her up and down. "And you?" He pointed a finger at her chest. "What do you have to say for yourself? We don't have to do this if you're not ready for it."

Sariah stood up as tall as she could muster and puffed

out her chest. She took a deep breath. "I'm ready," she told him. "I won't fail this time."

Gabe turned his head to the side and gave her a look that spoke more of pity than reassurance, but he nodded and let his hand drop. "So be it," he replied.

Their teacher returned to the middle of the room. He cleared his throat and smoothed his shirt with his hands, then carefully eyed them both.

"Let's get started, then, shall we?"

This time, both Sariah and Harvey gave him enthusiastic nods.

Gabe nodded as well. "Much better. This, I can work with." He started pacing and looked over both of his students. "Now, who knows what the plan is for this evening? What are we here for?"

Harvey's hand shot up fast. He had one of his big, dopey grins and was bouncing slightly, barely able to contain his excitement.

Gabe nodded at the younger man. "You can just speak, you know. There's only the three of us here. No need to raise your hand."

Harvey put his hand down and looked at the older man with a sheepish grin. "Right."

"Go ahead and share with the rest of the class."

Harvey beamed again. "Yes, sir!" He gave Gabriel a half-salute.

Sariah rolled her eyes. He was way too into all of this for her taste. Maybe it was a good thing and his enthusiasm could rub off on her.

The younger man cleared his throat loudly. "We're here to learn about physical magic this evening," he said with a smile. "Casting fireballs and moving things with your mind."

Gabe nodded again. "Good, good. Yes, you're correct, Harvey. One gold star for you."

Harvey shot him a dirty look. "Hey, I'm not some grade-schooler or something."

Gabe chuckled. "No, I guess not. Sorry, I'll keep it a bit more formal." He smoothed out another wrinkle in his shirt. "You are correct, at any rate. We're learning the basics of physical magic tonight. Who can tell me what that means, exactly?"

Harvey cocked his head to the side. "Beg pardon?"

Gabe sighed. "You know, what's the importance of physical magic? How does it differ from the other types? What are its strengths and limitations? That sort of thing."

"What does all that matter?" Harvey blurted out. "I just want to start killing things with my mind."

Their teacher sighed again, deeper this time. He shook his head, as well, then pulled on his face for good measure. "This is going to be harder than I thought," he muttered.

"Hey," Sariah chimed in. "He's just excited to start learning. What's so wrong about that?"

Gabe opened his mouth to argue, then shut it again just as quickly. "I..." He rubbed his chin and thought about it for a moment. "Huh."

"Huh what?" Harvey asked.

"I guess I don't really have an answer," Gabe replied with a grin. He threw his hands up in defeat. "Well enough. Let's just start with the basics, shall we?"

Harvey gave him another dopey grin. "Just show me how to cast a fireball already!"

Gabe rolled his eyes. "Easy, tiger. We're not going to start with moves like that. Not tonight."

"Aww, come on!" Harvey whined. "I can do it, I swear!"

The older man gave him a sideways glance. "You can, can you?"

Harvey nodded vigorously. "You bet I can."

"All right," he said. "If you're so sure of yourself, fine. I'll show you exactly how to cast a fireball."

"Yes!" Harvey raised his hands in the air in a victory pose. "Now, how do you do it?"

"Patience, kid, I'm getting to it." Gabe flexed his shoulders a couple times and stretched out his neck muscles by moving his head side to side, then put his hands together and pushed outwards to crack several knuckles at once.

Harvey watched it all very intently. "Is all that necessary, too?"

Gabe chuckled. "Sure, kid. Now watch this real closely. This is the most important part."

Harvey nodded and stared at the older man. Gabe made a fanning motion with his hands like he was trying to mimic the motion of a real fire, then clapped his hands together and pulled them slowly apart.

As his hands separated, a tiny spark of flame came to life in between them. It grew bigger as Gabe moved his hands further apart. Soon, Gabe had a fireball the size of a small cat in between his hands.

"Wow!" Harvey exclaimed, awestruck.

Gabe winked at him. "Impressive." He flicked his wrist and the fire died down to nothing in an instant.

"Yeah, yeah it really was," Harvey admitted. He had a greedy look in his eyes.

Gabe flashed the kid a devilish grin. "All right, now you give it a try."

Harvey rubbed his hands together. "I've got this!"

The younger man walked into the center of the room. He held out his arms to push Gabe and Sariah out of the way, so he'd have plenty of room to work. He started mimicking the motions he'd seen their teacher do.

He looked quite foolish stretching and pushing this way and that in vague power stances and waving his hands around.

Harvey clapped his hands together and pulled them apart just like Gabriel had done, but nothing happened. There was no fire. Only a kid with a bruised ego looking foolish.

Harvey's eyes fell to the floor. He tried the sequence of motions another time or two, thinking maybe he'd gotten them wrong, but still nothing happened.

Sariah looked from Harvey's downtrodden expression over to Gabe, who was grinning and snickering in the corner like a fool. She walked over and smacked the older man on the shoulder.

"Hey!" Gabe cried. He rubbed the spot on his arm where Sariah had hit him. "What was that for?"

The sound was enough to rouse Harvey from his concentration, and he looked at them, his previous failures momentarily forgotten.

"You knew all along it wouldn't work!" Sariah accused. She smacked Gabe on the chest for good measure.

"Ouch!" Gabe called back. He looked at her defiantly. "So what if I did? The kid's ego needed to get knocked down a peg or two if this training was going to get underway!"

"This kid?" Harvey repeated in an angry tone. He took a step toward Gabe.

Gabe backed up a half-step. It was clear he felt closed in with both of his students looking at him angrily.

He put his hands out defensively. "Okay, so maybe it wasn't the best thing to say just then," he admitted slowly. "I'm sorry, okay. I was just having a bit of fun."

Both Sariah and Harvey backed up to give him space.

Harvey stuck out his hand. "I'm sorry, too. I should have listened better."

Gabe took the offered hand and shook it. He stood up straighter and smoothed out his clothes again with his free hand. "Let's just get back to the training, shall we?"

Harvey nodded. "Sounds like a great plan."

Sariah agreed. "Yes, let's get back to the training. And real training, this time. No more games."

"Right," Gabe replied. "No more games."

Their teacher cleared his throat and returned to the middle of the room, turning to face them both one more time. "Now, do you want to know why the fireball spell worked for me, but it didn't work for Harvey?"

Both of them nodded.

Gabe grinned. "It's because the motions have nothing to do with the magic."

Harvey cocked his head to the side. "They don't?"

Gabe shook his head. "No, they don't."

"Then why did you-"

"Make all those motions all over the place in strange patterns?"

Harvey nodded.

"Mostly just to mess with you," Gabe admitted. "Mostly. To tell the truth, the motions have a little bit to do with the magic, but not in the way you think."

"Ugh," Sariah started. "Look, I appreciate the lecture, but don't we have better things to do than stand around all night listening to you prattle on about your magic knowledge? I thought we were going to learn some spells."

Gabe looked slightly wounded. "I was getting to that part, I swear!"

Sariah scoffed at him and folded her arms across her chest. "Yeah. In an hour."

"Hey!" Gabe replied.

She glared at him. "Seriously, dude. Two more minutes of this tops, then let's get to training, please?"

Gabe gave her a sheepish look and threw up his hands. "Sorry." He looked downtrodden for a second, then perked back up.

"As I was saying, physical magic is connected to your immediate environment, so some people use things like hand motions to help them center their power. It can be a useful tool to help you channel the magic, but the magic itself still comes from the nanocytes within you. Everything else is just window dressing. Never forget that part. The power comes from within."

"Now can we get to the actual training?" Sariah pleaded. "Please?"

"Right." Gabe rubbed his neck. "Yes, let's get to the training. For tonight's training, I've decided to start with a simple trick. Moving objects with your mind. It's one of the more basic ways to use physical magic, so it's good as a starting point."

As he spoke, he started rummaging through his pockets and extracting small objects that he placed gingerly on the floor.

Sariah gasped as she eyed the objects knowingly. "Are those...?"

"My special magic training stones you made fun of all those weeks ago?" Gabe replied. His cheeks burned a bright crimson. "Why yes, yes they are."

In spite of herself, Sariah started laughing, though inwardly, she was glad. If he was bringing his special little rocks out again, it meant he was taking her seriously this time. During their last training session, the stones had been conspicuously absent.

"You're not going to make us meditate again, are you?" she asked him.

Harvey looked at both of them, confused. "Am I missing something?"

Sariah stopped laughing long enough to look at him. "Careful, Harvey, or next thing you know, Gabe's going to have you thinking about his big, fat balls," she said with a grin plastered on her face.

She started laughing again. This time, Gabe joined in.

Harvey kept looking at both of them with a deadpan expression. "What's going on between you two? What did I miss?"

Sariah placed a hand on his shoulder and finally calmed down enough to talk. "Oh nothing, I promise." She winked at him. "Just a stupid joke from Gabe's earlier training session. You know, the one where he helped me find you and save your life?"

The whole room sobered up quickly. Harvey let the topic drop.

Gabe sighed and went back to placing his stones down on the floor like nothing had happened. "No, we're not going to use these to meditate," he said with half a grin, holding back another chuckle. "You're going to focus on moving these stones with magic."

"Any of them?" Harvey asked.

Gabe looked straight at him. "For you? Yes. Any of the stones. Just try to move one of them without touching it." Then he looked at Sariah. "But you? You get this stone." He shoved a tiny object into her hands.

Sariah looked down at the stone Gabe had given her. It was the stone with a crack in it. She fought back the urge to laugh again. "I should have known you'd give me this one."

Gabe flashed her a toothy smile. "Well, you showed such appreciation for it last time, I thought you'd like to take it for another spin."

She understood the message well enough. If she got too enthusiastic with this exercise and broke the stone, at least it would be the already broken one.

"And that's it," Gabe told them. He made a shooing motion with his hands. "Go ahead, get started."

"That's it?" Sariah repeated. "No words of advice or further pointers?"

Gabe shook his head. "Nope. That's really all I can tell you. The rest has to come from within you, remember?"

Sariah scowled and rolled her eyes, but didn't argue the point further.

Instead, she turned her attention to the rock in her hands. She rubbed her thumb along its edge, feeling the crack and remembering the earlier episode where she'd broken it.

She'd had doubts about her ability back then, and she'd proved herself well enough. She could do it again.

Sariah placed the rock on the ground in front of her. She fought against the urge to move it with her body and just tried to focus on the rock itself. The focus was essential to mental magic.

That spurred another thought. With mental magic, you didn't actually change anything, you just made it look like it had changed.

Perhaps physical magic worked the same way.

It was worth a shot, and it made the whole thing seem less icky somehow to liken it to something she knew. She imagined the rock five feet away from her on a different part of the floor. She focused on the thought as hard as she could. In spite of her effort, the rock didn't move an inch. It stayed exactly where it was.

Ugh, she thought. I guess maybe it's not so similar after all.

She kept at it. Instead of picturing the rock in a different spot, she tried picturing it flying through the air to that same spot and focused. Only, that didn't make a difference, either. Try as she might, the rock didn't budge.

She looked at Harvey. His rock was starting to teeter back and forth a little bit. It looked like her friend was getting the hang of this physical magic thing faster than she was.

That should have made her feel happy for him, but it only made her feel worse.

Gabe, meanwhile, was twirling one of the rocks in front of his face in a swirling pattern while wearing a smug grin. The little douche nugget. He was always so superior when he taught her.

She wanted nothing more than to pelt his face with the rock at her feet so bad she could almost taste it, just to wipe that stupid grin off his face.

She mimicked the motion of throwing the stone at his big head with one of her arms even though it had nothing in it and thought about how satisfying it would be to watch the rock smack into him. In her mind's eye, she saw it happen and it brought a smile to her face.

Not a moment later, the rock at her feet flew off the ground and zoomed right past Gabriel's face, missing it by a fraction of an inch.

Gabe's rock dropped to the ground and he blinked a couple of times. "Hey!" he shouted at Sariah. "What was that for?"

Sariah smiled. "I was only doing what you asked," she said demurely. "Besides, you never said where we were supposed to move your stupid rocks."

Gabe's jaw fell open and he raised his hands in an accusatory motion but let them drop. "I guess not." He grinned at her like an idiot. "So...how'd you do it?"

Her cheeks burned red and she shrugged her shoulders. "Honestly, I'm not sure. I just imagined I was throwing it and all of a sudden, the rock moved on its own."

"Want to give it another shot? See if it's a one-off?" Gabe offered.

Sariah rubbed her chin. "Are you sure? My aim could be better this time, you know," she replied with a smirk.

Gabe rolled his eyes. "Just do it already. I can defend myself. Promise."

"Okay, but I warned you."

Sariah thought about the rock again and thought about it flying back across the room and into her palm. As she did so, she made a beckoning motion with her fingers. For a moment, nothing happened, but as she concentrated on the motion of the rock, she heard something shift, then suddenly the rock flew back into her hand.

Just as quickly, she motioned for the rock to fly back at Gabriel. Once more, the rock obeyed her and flew past him, barely nicking his ear.

"Fantastic!" Gabe said with a grin. To his credit, he didn't seem phased by her aim in the slightest. "You're a natural at this, I tell you." He walked over and patted her on the back.

Sariah's cheeks burned even hotter. "Aww, I don't know about that."

"No seriously, you're pretty amazing at this 'magic-y stuff.'"

Sariah knew he was making fun of her when he said "magic-y stuff" like she did, but she didn't care. It was nice to hear praise coming from his mouth instead of disappointment.

She brushed a rogue strand of hair out of her face. "Yeah?"

Gabe looked at her. His eyes were practically sparkling in the dim light of the room. "Yeah," he said with a nod.

The two heard a loud crash from behind them and the sound of Harvey swearing.

"Scheisse, I'm sorry!" he called out.

Gabe and Sariah turned to look at the younger man. He was holding one of the stones in his hand and looking at them with one of his signature dopey grins.

Sariah squinted to look at the rock in his hands. It took a second, but before long she saw what was wrong. Harvey's rock, too, had a giant crack down the side of it.

Gabe pulled on his face and groaned. "Not again!"

CHAPTER FOUR

Gabe walked up to his room slowly. Harvey and Sariah were inside working on their magic training. He'd gone on a morning walk with Bear. He liked his morning walks. They were usually calm and serene. A chance to get away from it all and remember why he liked being alone.

I like being alone. Don't I?

He wasn't so sure anymore. Ever since Sariah had walked into his life, things had been in turmoil. He liked the girl, maybe more than he should. Not romantically or anything, but as a friend. At least, that's what he kept telling himself. He wasn't too sure about that anymore, either.

A sigh escaped his lips and he slumped his shoulders.

More importantly, Sariah gave him an opportunity to train the apprentice he'd always wanted. If he were honest with himself, Harvey wasn't half bad as a student, either. It was like two for the price of one - a deal too good to pass by.

Which was going to make what he had to do next that

much harder. Maybe that's why he was stalling and taking as much time during his morning walk as he had. He didn't want to break the news to his two promising students. It wasn't that he'd miss their company, it was that he didn't want to disappoint either of them.

Gabe raised his hand and gave the door four firm knocks in tight succession. It was his standard greeting. Days ago, they'd agreed on a specific knock pattern so they could know when it was one of them coming to the door versus someone else, like a maid. A minor precaution, but one that was necessary in his opinion.

"Who is it?" a voice came from within. It was Sariah.

Gabe rolled his eyes at the door as if the people within it could see his reaction. "Oh come on!" he growled. "You know damn well who it is."

He heard the sound of feet shuffling and a moment later the sound of someone tinkering with the door lock. The door was opened and Sariah's smiling face greeted him. Her eyes were gleaming in the harsh light of the hallway. If he wasn't careful, he could get used to being greeted like this.

"Just had to make sure," Sariah replied. "You can't be too careful these days. Someone could have copied our knock pattern or something."

Gabe sighed. "Hey! Quit poking fun at my security precautions. They're important," he whined.

Sariah chuckled and punched him lightly on the arm. "Just get in here already, you big lug."

Gabe rubbed his arm where Sariah had hit him and complied. Bear followed quickly after.

"There you are my good boy!" Sariah squealed when

she saw Bear. She reached down and took his head in her hands and started scratching and petting him. "You're such a good boy, yes, you are," she told the animal.

Bear barked at her in appreciation and licked her hands. The two of them kept it up for a solid minute before the dog settled down.

Gabe frowned. He was happy his dog loved his companions so much, but a little jealous at the same time. Bear was his dog, not hers. Even if the animal seemed to forget it from time to time.

He pulled out a strip of dried meat from one of his pockets and jiggled it in front of the dog. That got Bear running back to his side.

Bending, he rubbed Bear's big head, happy he could still bribe him with food.

Harvey came over. "Got any treats for the rest of us?" he asked with one of his signature grins.

Gabe looked at Harvey staring at him, mouth salivating much as Bear's had a moment earlier, and almost laughed out loud.

He shook his head. "Sorry, kid. Not this morning. Maybe next time, though."

Harvey looked downtrodden. "Aw, man. And we were working so hard this morning, too!"

Gabe tilted his head in Harvey's direction. "Yeah? Tell me more."

The younger man beamed at him. "We've been practicing our physical magic. I was able to conjure a small fireball a few hours ago."

"Really?" The corners of Gabe's lips curled into a smile.

"That's amazing." He pointed over at Sariah. "How's she doing?"

Harvey's face darkened and his tone dropped. "She's...doing great, too," he said.

Gabe smiled at him and sighed. The kid was trying to cover for her but doing a poor job at it. Sariah had shown considerable promise in the nighttime session a few days ago, but since then not so much. He wasn't sure if she wasn't pushing herself hard enough or if it really was hard for her to learn the physical stuff.

Harvey had the opposite problem. He'd picked up physical magic super quick, but mental was out of his reach.

He wondered if he was expecting too much from them. Magic had torn apart their entire world. That had to be hard to get over, even for someone as determined as Sariah.

He took a step forward and put a hand on her shoulder. "Heard you're doing great," he lied.

Sariah smiled weakly, then looked away. "Oh yeah. I'm doing freaking fantastic."

Gabe wanted to say something reassuring, to tell her he believed in her, and she was capable of greatness. Words failed him, so he just smiled instead.

"So how was your walk?" Harvey asked, breaking the awkward silence.

Gabe nodded at the kid. "Oh yeah. About that."

The two snapped to attention and looked at him intently. He supposed he deserved it. He usually never said much of anything about his morning walks, let alone leave it on a cliffhanger.

He took a deep breath to steady himself.

Now or never, I suppose.

"Well, you see, I ran into an old friend this morning."

"Yeah?" Harvey replied. "Anyone we know?"

Gabe shook his head. Of course not, he thought. Instead, he said, "No, I don't think so. They were from a long time ago."

Harvey nodded his head. "Awesome. So, when do we meet this friend of yours?"

Gabe was taken aback. That wasn't the answer he'd expected. "Never," he blurted out.

Sariah cocked her head to the side. "Never? That's harsh. Do we smell bad or something?" She sniffed herself as if to exemplify the point.

He backed up a step and put his hands out in front of him. "It's not like that," he stammered. "It's just...well, he couldn't stick around, you see. He had to run off."

"Oh," Sariah and Harvey replied in unison.

"Right. Anyway, he wanted me to go with him. I told him I could do no such thing." He waved his hands in a dismissive gesture for emphasis.

"Why would you go and say a thing like that?" Harvey inquired.

Gabe gave a weak laugh. "For you guys, of course. I need to watch after both of you." He looked at the ground and shuffled his feet. "Even if it would only be for a few days."

Harvey scoffed and rolled his eyes. "You worry too much. We'd be fine for a couple of days. What trouble could we possibly get into, anyway?"

Gabe opened his mouth to remind the younger man that the last time he'd been left alone he'd managed to get himself kidnapped but decided against it. "I guess you're right."

The boy nodded. "We wouldn't mind, would we, Sariah?" He nudged her arm. "We'll just be here training anyway."

Sariah side-eyed the kid and huffed. "Of course," she said quickly. "What else would we do?"

Gabe didn't like her answer one bit. It was far too open-ended, but he let it go. It wouldn't do him any good to get into an argument with her now. He had to get going or he'd be late.

"If you're sure you're both okay with it."

Harvey nodded again. "We're sure."

"All right." Gabe shrugged. "I guess I'll tell my friend that I changed my mind."

Gabe smiled at his two students. This conversation couldn't have gone better if he'd planned it. He whistled to Bear. "Come on, boy."

In response, the dog walked over to Sariah and wrapped himself up at her feet. Gabe shook his head. He'd been betrayed yet again.

Sariah gave Bear another scratch behind his ears and called him a good boy.

Is that her secret weapon? he wondered. He'd done the same thing several times and Bear never seemed to reply that way to him.

With a heavy sigh, he turned and left the room, hoping his students would be true to their word and stay out of trouble.

Sariah glanced over at Harvey. He had an odd look. Not quite one of his grins but almost.

She gave him a half-smile and he smirked at her like an idiot. It was nearing midday and they'd been alone almost the whole morning, like most mornings for the past couple of days, she supposed.

Neither of them had said anything practically the whole time. There were tons of things they could be talking about, heck, needed to talk about, but they barely ever said a word to each other during these "practice times." Instead they just concentrated and focused on the magic.

Now she was facing the prospect of a few more days of just this with no Gabe to mix it up. She shook her head. It was unbearable. At least when Gabe was around, she could break the monotony by teasing him about something.

Harvey looked at her again. His demeanor shifted until there was an inquisitive look in his eyes. "What are you thinking about?" he asked.

The suddenness of his question took her back and she shuddered. She shrugged her shoulders. "Nothing," she lied.

Sariah sighed. Men can be so dense. There was a lot going on inside her mind, just nothing she wanted to vocalize.

"Okay," he replied and gave her a wink. He went back to concentrating on the stones on the ground in front of him.

She supposed she should be happy she'd gotten that much out of him. Ever since their near kiss at the Dusk Raven stronghold a few weeks ago, Harvey had been tight-lipped, and barely ever said a thing.

We used to talk all the time, she mused. What changed?

She still didn't know why he'd acted that way. Was he starting to develop feelings for her? If he was, she didn't have time to be embroiled in a relationship right now.

It would be great if Harvey would at least say something about the incident, but it was no use. He was closed off and magic training had only made him more tight-lipped.

She watched him juggle his pile of stones in the air for a moment to clear her head. He was getting pretty good at manipulating them with his mind and arranging them into various patterns.

Better than she was if she was honest about it. Why is this so hard for me?

Growling, she turned her attention back to the pile of rocks at her feet. She was supposed to be manipulating them with her mind and moving them into a pattern. It was the practice task Gabe had set for them.

The trick was easy enough and required little effort, but it did little to quell the sense of unease growing in her gut.

For the past three weeks now, she'd done little but hang around Stratton and play with these rocks. Meanwhile, the Master and his Dusk Ravens were out there getting stronger by the day.

What was their next move? When would he come for her? Would she be ready? She had no answers. Only a pile of rocks that were hers to command.

What good is this going to do me when the time comes? she huffed.

She needed a change of pace, something to get her out of her slump, and off of thinking about how stupid the men in her life were.

An idea struck her - what she needed was a competition.

Sariah's eyes gleamed and a smile crept up on her face. A competition! She and Harvey would have them all the time growing up. They always helped her stretch herself and it was better than waiting for him to stop being a dunderhead.

All she needed was to convince him of the same. She looked at Harvey and gave him a light shove on the arm. It was just enough to make him break his concentration and his stones went hurtling in every direction.

"Hey!" Harvey grumbled. "What was that for?"

Sariah gave him a sheepish grin and lowered her head. "Sorry, I didn't think my little touch would mess up your spell like that."

Harvey frowned. "No, it's okay. To be honest, I'm not sure why it bugged me so much, anyway." He flashed her a grin. "Guess I need to learn to use magic while distracted."

"Oh? Am I distracting, then?" Sariah batted her eyes.

He waved a hand dismissively. "Of course not! I mean, uh ...no you're fine." He grinned at her again, but the smile looked slightly fake.

"Anyway, you were bragging to Gabriel earlier today about your progress," Sariah told him.

He shrugged. "I was just telling him about my accomplishments."

She nodded. "Uh-huh. The way I heard it, you've succeeded at everything while I'm barely even trying."

Harvey raised his hands defensively. "Look, Sariah. You've been doing great with the rocks, but it feels like you don't even want to attempt a fireball." He looked down at her and patted her shoulder. "You need to learn to apply yourself more fully."

She bit her lip involuntarily. He really thought she wasn't applying herself. It wasn't that, it was just she wasn't getting it as fast as she wanted to.

She felt heat rise to her brain and let herself take the bait. "Pfft. What's that supposed to mean?"

"I'm not sure how to put this into words. To be honest, Sariah, I'm worried about you."

"You? Worried about me?" She shot him an icy glare. "I assure you, you have nothing to worry about."

He rubbed his chin. "Oh, I believe you. It's just I don't want to see you start falling behind, is all."

Sariah scoffed. He had a really low opinion of her skills.

"Falling behind? Behind what? You and your stupid rock art?" She grunted and folded her arms over her chest.

Harvey put his hands out defensively. "Now, now. I didn't mean it like that."

Well, this wasn't going as planned, she mused. She should have known better.

"So what is it, then?" she asked. "You think you're better than me?"

Harvey puffed up his chest. He nodded. "I guess you could say that. Yeah, yeah I am better at physical magic than you."

Now, this I can work with, she thought triumphantly.

"That so?" She rubbed her chin. "Care to make a wager? Put your money where your mouth is?"

Harvey gave her a smirk. "Why yes, as a matter of fact, I would."

Sariah nodded. "Good. Let's get going, then."

She turned and started heading out the door. Bear followed suit.

Harvey's jaw dropped to the floor. "Wait a second!" he called after her. "Where are we going?"

She turned and smiled at him. "You'll see soon enough."

Sariah raced through the streets of the city of Stratton with Harvey and Bear close on her heels. Harvey had tried to get information out of her a couple of times, but she'd remained tight-lipped about the whole thing.

She could have told him about her plan, she supposed, but that would spoil some of the fun.

Pretty soon, the two were walking past the front gates to the city. Sariah looked around and spotted the guard Sergeant Ty Genrose who had been there the last two times she'd come across the gate.

She wondered briefly if that was the friend Gabe had spoken of earlier. The two of them had more shared history than Gabe had let on. Of that, she was certain, though she didn't know any more about it. In all their conversations, Gabe had never said a single word about the man.

Nah. If Gabe had been off to see Ty, the sergeant wouldn't still be standing at the gate. Gabe must be seeing someone else.

It was possible Ty would know who that someone was, but even if he did, it was unlikely he'd say anything about it even if pressed.

She bit her lip and thought about going and asking him

anyway, but decided against it. She'd just pester Gabe when he got back. She was getting very effective at pestering him for information.

She gave Ty a nod of recognition and kept walking out of the city gates.

Harvey pulled on her shoulder to stop her. He was breathing hard. "Wait a second," he said in between breaths.

It wasn't until then she realized just how fast she'd been going. Apparently fast enough Harvey was out of breath trying to keep up with her.

"Where do you think you're going, exactly?" he demanded.

Sariah gave him a giant smile. "Out of town, silly." She pointed at the giant gates to the city. "I figured that much was obvious."

Harvey frowned. "But why?"

"So we can have our little contest, of course."

"Out here?" Harvey whined. His eyes darted around. "Why does it have to be outside of town." The last part he said in a hushed tone as though he was afraid of something. "You do remember what happened last time we were out here, don't you?"

Sariah patted him on the chest. "I remember we made it out just fine in the end."

Harvey nodded. "Yeah, but with Gabe's help."

She gave him a light shove. "True, but neither of us had physical magic back then. We're not sitting ducks anymore."

Harvey rubbed his chin. "I suppose you have a point. Still..."

"Still what?"

He blinked. "Well, it's just we swore we'd stay out of trouble while Gabe was gone and—"

Sariah gave him a wry smile. "And we will. It's just a little contest. It's not like we're going on a rampage."

"I suppose you have a point. I just don't know."

"Besides," she continued, "no one's seen the Dusk Ravens since we burned down their camp. There's nothing out here to be worried about."

He tilted his head back a bit thinking hard on something. "I guess there's nothing to be concerned about." He paused for a second. "But if Gabe finds out—"

"Gabe won't know if we don't tell him," Sariah assured him. She waved her hand dismissively. "Come on. It'll be fun."

Harvey still looked doubtful, but eventually he nodded. "Okay, if you say so."

Sariah eyed him up and down. "I'm glad you see it my way for a change." She pointed. "Shall we?"

Harvey said nothing and with that, the three continued their trek outside the city of Stratton.

A short way past the gates, Sariah veered hard to the left. A small wooded area off in the distance was her target. It was relatively close to the gates and the safety of the giant city.

Not that the city was all that safe, either, when she thought about it. Harvey had been kidnapped in the middle of the street in the waning hours of daylight and no one had so much as stopped to say anything.

Still, that was before they'd attacked the bandit encampment west of here. The damage they'd caused to the camp had been pretty severe, and not much had been heard about them since.

Sariah took a few more steps forward and felt a shiver across her spine. It was midday, and the sun was beating down on them, so it wasn't because it was cold.

She wondered if there was something to be worried about out there. She shook her head to clear it of such thoughts. Harvey's jumpiness was getting to her. There was nothing out there but grass and a small outcropping of trees.

A few moments later, they reached their destination. Sariah walked up to one of the trees and took out the dagger she always carried with her. She stuck it into the tree and started carving out a small pattern.

"What are you doing to that tree?" Harvey objected.

"I'm making a target on it, of course."

Harvey furrowed his brow. "A target?"

She nodded. "Yeah, you know. A target. Like the thing you try to hit when you're throwing weapons or shooting a bow."

Harvey's eyes darted around. "Are you sure you should be doing that? Someone might own this tree and take offense."

Sariah scoffed. "Do you see anyone around here?" She pointed her finger. "No? I didn't think so. Trust me, we'll be just fine."

Harvey gave her a look that said he disapproved, but he dropped the subject.

Soon enough, the deed was done. She took a step back to admire her handiwork. Her target was crude, but it was small and would do the job.

"Now can you tell me what all this is about?" Harvey inquired.

Sariah grinned at him. "This is for our wager. We're going to use our magic to try and hit this target from way over there." She pointed to a distant spot. "Whoever ends up closer is the winner." She was quite proud of this idea.

Harvey rubbed his chin. "Okay, that's fair. I can handle that."

"I thought you'd see it my way."

"And totally crush you in the process," he added with a slight jab at her chest.

Sariah's smile got even broader. "Now that's the Harvey I love so much. Where have you been, by the way?" She gave him a wink.

Harvey grinned back at her with his big, signature dopey grin and the two stared at each other for a moment before anyone did anything. Then he broke into a run toward the spot Sariah had pointed at.

"Race you!" he called out behind him.

Sariah growled a little and chased after him. It felt good to be competing with Harvey like this, even if he was cheating. It felt like old times back in Chatwick before her world had been turned upside down.

Try though she might, Harvey beat her handily. Technically Bear beat both of them. He bounded past them both and stood on the designated spot barking his victory for all the world to hear while they caught up to him. It made Sariah chuckle.

After the three had sufficient time to stop and catch their breath, Sariah pulled another dagger out of her pocket and handed the blade to Harvey.

"Here," she said.

Harvey took the offered blade with an odd expression. "What's this for?"

"For the contest, dummy. We're going to use our magic to throw these knives and try to hit the target."

Harvey tilted his head to the side. "Knives?" he repeated.

"What? You didn't think we'd use more rocks, did you?" Sariah chuckled. "I don't know about you, but I've had just about all the rocks I can handle after the last couple of days."

Harvey nodded slowly. "Fair point. Okay. We'll do it your way."

"Of course, we will," she replied with a grin.

She made a broad-sweeping motion with her hands. "Here. You can even go first."

Harvey gave her a slight bow. "Why how generous, milady."

"Oh, you know me. Generous to a fault."

That made Harvey laugh a little, and Sariah joined in for a second before they both calmed back down.

Harvey set his knife down on the ground before him. "This way you know I'm not cheating," he explained.

Sariah nodded. She didn't really think he'd try to cheat at this one anyway. He had too much pride to do something like that.

Harvey cracked his knuckles once and got to concentrating. His face hardened and he closed his eyes for a half-second. When they opened, they were coal black. He made a rising motion with his left hand and the blade in the grass lifted up slowly until it was level with his outstretched hand.

Then, Harvey pointed at the tree with the little target carved into it. In the same instant, the blade shot forth and cut through the air at lightning speed. A moment later, its point was buried into the side of the tree inches from the center of the target.

Sariah gave off a low whistle. "Mighty impressive," she admitted. In truth, she really was impressed. She hadn't expected him to even hit the tree.

Maybe he's better at this whole physical magic-y thing than I thought.

Harvey nodded at her. "Your turn."

"Stand back," she insisted and Harvey obliged.

She placed her own knife in the grass as Harvey had done and took a wide stance, then fanned out her hands in front of her. She tried to calm her mind as best she could and center her thoughts so she could summon her own magic. She wasn't about to be outdone by Harvey's little performance.

When she opened her own eyes, they were coal black as well. She focused intently on the knife and made a beckoning motion with her hand. The knife lifted itself effortlessly into the air.

Sariah let the knife hang in the air for a moment and spun it around until it was pointed at the tree.

She gritted her teeth and prepared herself to send the blade flying. She rolled her shoulders one time and pushed forward with one hand. The dagger obeyed her command and started flying.

When the blade was about halfway to its target, she

heard a blood-curdling scream in the distance. The sound jolted her concentration and the knife spun out of control. It flew well past the marked tree and landed somewhere off in the distance beyond where she couldn't see it.

Sariah frowned and looked at Harvey. "I thought you said you weren't going to cheat," she whined.

Harvey gave her a quizzical look. "What do you mean?"

"Oh come on! You screamed like a little girl and distracted me, making me miss the target."

Harvey shot her a confused look. "That wasn't me! I have no idea what that was, but I didn't do it." He put a hand on her shoulder. "Look, you can try again, okay?"

Sariah was about to nod when the scream came again, sounding more urgent this time.

Both of them turned to look. "Someone's in trouble!" Harvey shouted.

Sariah's blood chilled. Someone out there needed help, and they were the only ones in the vicinity. But they were mere students. What could they do to help? There was only one right answer.

"Help is on the way!" Sariah screamed, sparing a glance at Harvey. She bounded off in the direction of the scream, not waiting to see if Harvey followed.

CHAPTER FIVE

Sariah ran as fast as she could. The scream they'd heard had come from over the next rise. She was sure of it, and even though she didn't have any idea what was waiting for her, someone out there needed help.

I should have waited for Harvey and Bear, she thought, chewing on her lip. Or at least slowed down to save some energy, but as usual she'd rushed forward. Shrugging, she bounded forth as fast as her feet would take her over the field.

When she reached the crest of the hill, she stopped for a brief second to catch her breath. The scream came again, even louder than last time.

She rounded the top of the little hill and took in the scene in front of her. About a hundred meters in front of her was a lone merchant with a couple of horses and a big cart. Sariah couldn't tell what was in the cart from this distance, but it looked to be full of goods. No doubt the merchant had been headed toward Stratton to try and sell her wares when she'd been attacked.

The merchant had a small knife in her hands she was using to try and ward off her attackers.

There were three of them, and they obviously had the upper hand. Two of the attackers, one male and one female, were armed with swords, and the third one had a rather cruel-looking mace he was holding menacingly out in front of him.

Mace guy would occasionally make a swipe at the poor woman merchant with his massive weapon, and she'd back up with each advance. Not that she had much further to go before she'd be completely out of room.

Fortunately, none of them seemed to have noticed Sariah's arrival, which meant she had the benefit of surprise on her side, which she'd need if she wanted to make a difference.

Sariah's hand tightened around the hilt of the sword hanging at her side. She figured she could descend on them, sword arm swinging from behind and probably take out one of them before the bandits even knew what hit them.

That would still leave two of them to attack her afterward, and from the looks of things, she couldn't count on the merchant for any help. That left her with bad odds.

She mentally chided herself for not waiting longer to make sure Harvey and Bear had been with her before running off.

After grimacing for a moment, Sariah decided to use magic. If she could fell two of them with a fireball before they reached her, it evened the odds. The only problem was she'd never summoned forth a fireball before, let alone two.

I can do this, she thought. She took in a deep breath to calm her thoughts. This is what I've been training for, to protect people. I have to do this.

That thought made her feel more confident. She shook out her hands and closed her eyes, focusing on the thought of fire. Its heat, its intensity, its destruction.

When she opened her eyes to find a target, she felt certain she could manage the feat. She picked Mace guy as her first. That weapon of his looked nasty, and she had no desire to be in close quarters with it. Taking him out was the first priority.

She put her hands together and slowly pulled them apart, concentrating on the thought of fire.

Even though she knew the actual motions meant nothing, it comforted her to use the same ones Gabe had used in his example.

It took a moment before anything happened, then all at once she felt a strong heat coming from something in between her palms. She looked down and there it was, a fireball. She'd done it.

Cocking her arm, she thrust it forward with all her might and the fireball went flying. It careened right into her chosen victim.

Sariah smiled. She'd managed a small victory. Now all she needed was to do it again.

Her excitement was short-lived. She watched in horror as the fireball came into contact with Mace guy's clothing and petered out a second later. His clothes looked singed, perhaps, but he was no worse for the wear.

Worse, he was now aware of her presence and more than a little pissed about it.

Sariah squeaked and looked Mace guy in the eyes. He growled at her and motioned for his two cronies to turn their attention to their new attacker as well.

A knot of fear formed in Sariah's chest. She was in for it now. The element of surprise was gone, and she still had all three attackers alive and well to chase her down.

She gulped down her fear and drew her blade from its sheath, trying to look sure and steady to hopefully put her attackers off their game.

It didn't work.

They moved on her at a medium clip, closing the distance quickly. They were maybe only thirty meters away now.

Sariah said a quick prayer in her head to the Matriarch and the Patriarch that she would come out of this okay. Then she did the only sensible thing she could think of. She ran.

Harvey growled. He retrieved their knives and started running. Sariah had taken off on him again, trying to play savior. He wasn't sure exactly, only that she was gone and there was some unknown danger out there.

The whole scene felt all too familiar. He was going to have strong words with her when he finally found her.

He heard the scream from before again. It was coming from off to his left, and he was pretty sure that was the direction Sariah had headed off to.

Harvey looked down at his side. Bear was right there,

matching him stride for stride. At least the animal hadn't abandoned him.

Bear gave him a knowing yelp and pointed his nose in the direction of the scream. Harvey nodded at the beast, and the two kept running.

A moment later, he heard the distinctive sound of Sariah squeaking. The blood chilled in his veins. She only made that noise when she was really in trouble.

Harvey followed the direction of the squeak, running even faster. He was determined to catch up and save her before it was too late.

He wondered how he would explain things to Gabriel if he let anything happen to Sariah while the older man was gone. He shook his head and decided the only answer was to make sure nothing happened to begin with.

He gritted his teeth and kept going.

Pretty soon, he came across the scene of a female merchant with an oversized cart and a couple of startled horses. The merchant looked at her would-be savior and pointed to the left.

Harvey nodded his thanks and kept going.

Sariah looked over her shoulder. All three attackers were following her. None of them had stayed to harass the merchant.

Which, she supposed, made a certain amount of sense. They could come back and take care of the merchant easily enough once she herself was taken care of. She might have done the same thing if their positions were reversed.

Since they weren't, she was running for her very life.

Sariah stole another glance over her shoulder. Her attackers were gaining on her, with only fifteen meters between them now.

She tried to think fast. She needed a new plan, a distraction so she could split up the attackers and take them out one at a time, but there was nothing out here to help her. She was in the middle of an empty field, and there wasn't even a house in sight for at least another two hundred meters. By that point, she'd be done for.

Another glance told her Mace guy and his cronies were only a few meters away now.

Running low on both time and options, she did the only thing left she could think of - she screamed and fell onto the ground head-first.

She tumbled around but managed to keep a hold of her sword in the process.

Her attackers hadn't expected her to do something so stupid, so they ended up overshooting her and then had to take extra time turning around to face her.

That small amount of extra time wasn't much, but it gave her a chance to strike first.

While still on the ground, she lashed out with her blade. It bit into mace guy's foot.

He howled and backed up, which allowed Sariah to get back to her feet before the two sword-wielders closed in.

She spared half a glance at Mace guy. He was wounded and moving slowly. She let out a deep breath. It was a small advantage, but it was more than she'd had before.

Now all she had to do was take out the other two

without dying before Mace guy got up the courage to come after her again.

Here goes nothing, she thought.

Sword woman made a swipe at her midsection which Sariah easily parried, but Sword guy followed up with a swipe of his own that she had much more trouble dodging.

The two attackers managed to force her backward a couple of steps. Then, with her energy waning and her focus diverted, she took a wrong step and tumbled over backward, spilling onto the ground once more.

She heard Sword woman laugh and watched as Mace guy seemed to shake off the pain and head her way, too.

Sword guy raised his blade high over his head like he was going to kill her with one swift stroke.

Sariah closed one eye and turned her head, waiting for the blow to come.

Harvey heard Sariah screaming not far off in front of him. He gritted his teeth. He was on the right track.

"I'm coming!" he shouted, but he was shouting into the wind and doubted anyone would hear him.

The crest of a hill rose just in front of him. Likely, Sariah was right on the other side.

He redoubled his efforts and as he rounded the top of the rise, he saw his worst fears come to life in front of him.

Sariah was there, all right, and had three attackers closing in on her - a sword woman, a sword guy, and mace-wielder.

Mace guy seemed to be limping, but no worse for the wear.

Harvey bit his lip. He was still a short way from the three of them, and they were closing in on her fast. He didn't have long.

He would need to use magic. He gulped down his emotions and willed his heart to slow down a half-step. He would need to concentrate if he was going to pull this off.

Using all the inner strength he could muster, he conjured forth a fireball. Then he looked at his opponents again. Sword guy had his blade up over his head like he was going to put an end to Sariah right then and there. That was the immediate threat.

He sent the fireball flying toward Sword guy as fast he could make it go.

Seconds later, Sword guy's clothes erupted into flames and he fell to the ground screaming.

Harvey smiled. The immediate threat was quelled, but there were still two more attackers and they would be alerted to his presence now.

One of the attackers, Mace guy, turned his focus to the new threat and came marching for him, but Sword woman seemed intent on taking out Sariah.

Thinking fast, Harvey took a dagger out of a sheath on his belt and used his magic to propel it forward. It struck Sword woman square on the hand.

The woman hissed in pain and dropped her sword. Harvey smiled again. That was two threats down, and only one left to go. And it was headed right this way.

At his side, he heard Bear give off a shrill bark. The dog was bounding toward Mace guy.

"Hey, wait for me!" Harvey cried. Then he chased after the animal.

———

Sariah heard the sound of fire erupt overhead and the sound of Sword guy screaming in pain and falling to the ground.

She opened her eyes fully. To her surprise, she was still very much alive. Sword guy? Not so much.

Even better, Sword woman seemed to be distracted and had somehow dropped her weapon.

Sariah didn't need further convincing. She got up and grabbed her blade tight, holding it out in front of her, and waited for Sword woman to come at her again.

It didn't take long. Sword woman produced another blade quickly enough and came for her, starting out with a low swipe toward Sariah's legs.

Sariah dodged backward a half-step and lashed out with her own blade, going for an upward-angled blow to her opponent's sword arm. It missed, but it kept her attacker from fully closing the distance.

Then Sariah followed up that swipe with a broad swing to Sword woman's middle and was parried easily enough.

Sword woman followed up with a quick succession of blows from every angle, which Sariah barely managed to fend off.

Sariah bent down and tried a desperate lunge at Sword woman's outstretched leg. This time, the blade connected, and the woman fell over.

With a quick swipe across Sword woman's back, Sariah

then plunged her blade through the back of the attacker's rib cage, piercing the woman's heart.

Panting, she took a half-second to admire her handiwork, then looked around to see what had become of Mace guy.

She didn't need to look far. Harvey and Bear were at the top of the hill, standing over Mace guy's corpse.

It was hard to tell for sure from this distance, but it looked like Bear had torn his throat out.

Sariah frowned. That was a tough way to go, even for bandit scum. She could almost feel for the guy. Almost.

"Fancy meeting you here," Sariah called out to Harvey.

Harvey smiled down at her. "Yeah, fancy that. Who'd have thought we'd meet all the way out here in the middle of nowhere?"

Sariah walked over to Harvey and gave him a giant hug. Her hands were shaking from the stress and the adrenaline of the battle.

He seemed shocked by the motion at first but hugged her back. She let herself be wrapped in his warmth for a moment before doing anything else.

She had to admit, it felt good being held by him like this, even if the circumstances were less than ideal. At least he was paying attention to her again.

"Thank you," she whispered.

Harvey patted her gently on the back. "Don't mention it. We're even now, yeah?"

Sariah nodded. "Yeah, I guess we kind of are."

Bear barked at both of them. Sariah looked down at the big dog, crouched down, and gave him a big hug as well. "Of course, you were also a big help, you mangy mutt," she told the animal. She gave him a good scratch behind the ears.

"We're going to have to figure out how to get all that blood off you, you know," she added.

Bear just barked in response.

Sariah gave her body another moment to calm down and for her hands to stop shaking before doing anything else, then she started rummaging around on the bandit's bodies.

Harvey frowned at her. "What are you doing, Sariah?"

"I'm looking for something," she replied cryptically.

She turned over both of Mace guy's hands. There on the right palm was what she was looking for - a small raven tattoo. The guy was a Dusk Raven. Undoubtedly, they all were.

Sariah scowled. The Dusk Ravens were starting up their activity in this area again. Either that, or it was a rogue band. She supposed it didn't matter. The only good Dusk Raven was a dead one.

She spat on Mace guy's corpse for good measure, then took his weapon and rifled through his clothes for any spare coins. She repeated the process with the other two bodies. None of them had much on them, but she came back with a handful of money and some fresh new weapons.

Harvey looked dumbfounded throughout the whole thing. "Why are you defiling their bodies?"

Sariah's cheeks flushed a bright crimson. "Is that what you think I'm doing?" she demanded. "Do you really think they were any nicer to their victims, this Dusk Raven scum?"

"I guess not." Harvey shook his head.

"If anything, I'm probably showing them more respect than they do to their victims. Besides, we could use all the supplies we can get for the battles that lay ahead. Can't rely on Gabe's goodwill all the time, can we?"

Harvey frowned. "How are we going to explain all the new weapons to him?"

Sariah shrugged her shoulders. "Who says we have to? Once they are cleaned, I'm sure we can pawn them off to a merchant in town. Then it's just a couple of extra coins, and those are easy enough to hide from view."

Harvey's head bobbed from side to side. "I guess you have a point. Still, it just seems so ..."

"Wrong?" Sariah finished for him. He nodded. "Then don't help me. I'll do it all myself. But ask yourself, would they show you the same courtesy if the tables were turned?"

Harvey sighed. "No, they sure wouldn't. You're right."

Sariah grinned at him. "I knew you'd see it my way eventually." She pointed back the way they'd come. "Now let's go see if that merchant is okay."

"Merchant?" Harvey asked. "Oh yeah, I passed one on the way to save you."

"Save me?" Sariah repeated. "Nonsense. I totally had them in the bag. I was just playing with them first." She gave him a friendly wink.

"Oh right." Harvey scratched his head, which made her chuckle. "Totally had them the whole time. What was I thinking?"

He pulled on her arm to stop her. "Seriously, why didn't you use magic to take them out like I did?"

Sariah blushed and turned her head away. "I did, sort of," she admitted. "It just wasn't quite as effective as yours was."

"Okay, I won't press you any further on it, but when we get back to town, you need to let me help you, okay? I'm sure we can overcome whatever your current issue is together."

"I'd like that," she said slowly.

The three of them kept walking, not saying anything to one another for several more minutes.

Before long, they came across the female merchant, who seemed all too happy to see them, if a little surprised.

Sariah offered her hand in greeting. "Hi. I'm Sariah. Nice to meet you."

The merchant scraped a bow, then took the offered hand. "My name is Darla. I am honored to accept your assistance in the earlier scuffle."

Sariah almost snorted. That's what this Darla person referred to as a "scuffle?" She had barely come out of it with her neck. It was a bit more than a scuffle.

She took back her hand. "When we heard your screams for help, we came right away. Really, it was the least we could do."

Darla looked confused. "But you do not know me. Why would you risk your lives for someone you have never even met before?"

Sariah shrugged. "It was the right thing to do."

Darla didn't seem convinced. "If you say so, my lord and lady. At any rate, I am most grateful for the aid." She bowed again, even grander this time.

Sariah blushed and tried to hide it. Darla was making

her feel very uncomfortable. She waved her off. "Aww, it was nothing. Anyone would have done the same thing," she insisted.

Darla shook her head. "Oh, I do not think so."

The merchant woman reached into her clothing. A moment later, she produced a couple of gold coins. "Here," she said, holding them out to Harvey and Sariah.

Harvey put his hands forward to accept the reward, but Sariah pushed them back.

"We couldn't possibly accept payment for doing the right thing, Darla," Sariah explained.

Darla bowed again. "If you are sure, my lord and lady." She put the coins back from where they'd come.

The merchant woman stared at the two like she was expecting them to say something else.

"Um, your thanks is more than enough?" Harvey stammered. He managed a slight bow as well, trying to mimic Darla's odd behavior.

A big smile crept over Darla's lips and she bowed deeply once more. That seemed to satisfy her. "Thank you again, kind lord and lady."

The merchant woman turned and went back to her horses. In the "scuffle," they had come unhitched from the cart.

Sariah took a step forward. "Please," she offered. "Let us help you with the horses as well. It's the least we can do."

Darla's cheeks grew a bright crimson. "Surely this kindness is too much, my lord and lady. I cannot accept."

"Nonsense," Harvey told her. "We'll have you back on your way in a jiffy. We'll even walk you the rest of the way to Stratton to make sure nothing happens."

Darla replied with yet another bow. This was getting ridiculous, but Sariah didn't know how to make her stop.

With the three of them working together, they managed to get the horses back on the hitch in no time, then all of them walked beside the cart as they made their way toward Stratton and safety.

Sariah laughed to herself. How odd that she thought of Stratton as a safe place now, when only a month prior it had seemed foreign and dangerous.

Time sure does change things.

She looked overhead. The sun was starting to get low against the horizon. It was well into the afternoon and it would be dusk in another hour or two. It was probably a good thing they were on their way back. She was suddenly feeling vulnerable out in the open.

The rest of the trip to Stratton passed without incident, and before long they were back at the city gates, only a little worse for the wear.

The gate guard Ty Genrose wasn't there this time. No doubt he'd turned in for the day. Sariah frowned. She really had to come back and pester him for information at some point in case her efforts with Gabe failed. It could wait for later.

Once they were within the city limits, they said their goodbyes to Darla.

Harvey gave her a small bow, and Darla gave a deep one in return. Sariah hugged her instead, which seemed to shock her all the more. Sariah had never really been one for much formality. She preferred a more personal approach.

Before she left, Darla said the strangest thing. "May the eagle rise over the hills when we meet again."

Neither Sariah nor Harvey could make heads or tails of it. They both scratched their heads and shrugged their shoulders and gave her a rather standard goodbye in comparison.

By then it was getting well and truly dark out. Not willing to waste any more time, Bear, Sariah, and Harvey headed back to The Dragonfly. When they got there, they collapsed onto their beds and fell fast asleep.

CHAPTER SIX

Severin scowled and kept walking. He passed a small dog and hissed to scare it away. The act felt good and right to him somehow, but the feeling passed quickly.

"Humph," he muttered.

The last place he wanted to be was exactly where he was headed. The Stratton merchant operations were already on thin ice after the surprise attack had ravaged half of his camp and set his supplies ablaze. He hadn't had time to replace them all yet.

To make matters worse, just yesterday he'd received a report of three bandit operatives in the region who had failed to report in at their regularly scheduled check-in time. That couldn't be good.

He suspected the girl from the previous attack had something to do with it, but he had no proof nor any real reason to think so outside of a nagging hunch. No one messed with the Dusk Ravens in broad daylight. No one but that stupid girl that is. What did the Master say her name was? He couldn't remember.

It didn't matter. The dumb bitch had gotten the drop on him and gotten lucky once. But only once. That kind of luck would only take someone so far.

When you've been in the game for as long as I have, you see some weird shit, he thought as he kept walking.

It was true. He'd seen multiple attempts at dethroning the Dusk Ravens or upsetting their power base. Every now and then, someone would get lucky and make some headway - like that stupid girl had. Eventually they all ended up the same way - with the Dusk Ravens on top and the other party dead.

He let those thoughts ruminate in his mind as he walked.

None of what happened would have been a big deal on its own, but now the Master had taken an interest. That was different. The Master was typically aloof. He stayed by himself and ruled from afar, interjecting his special talents only when necessary. This situation definitely didn't call for it, at least not yet.

Severin scowled. Why was the Master so interested in that stupid girl? What could she have possibly done to have forced the Master's hand and made him call an audience of all his top generals, something Severin could only remember happening three times before in the last fifteen years?

He was obviously overreacting. It was the only answer that made sense.

Not that Severin was going to ignore the call, even if the Master was foolish. There was no surer shortcut to ending up the subject of one of the Master's experiments than disobedience. Everyone knew that.

In spite of himself, he shuddered thinking of the Master's magical experiments. He was glad no one was around to notice. It wouldn't do to show even the slightest hint of weakness this close to the Master's inner chambers. He knew nothing about the experiments personally, only what he'd heard second-hand, but even that was enough to turn a priest to drink.

Severin had never really been interested in magic. He knew it was the source of the Master's power - him and a handful of his disciples - but personally he couldn't stomach the stuff. It wasn't natural. No, good steel and the power of his own two hands were all he'd needed to get to his current position. That was good enough for him.

A moment later, he was at the doorway to the stronghold proper. It was underground tunnels from here on out.

Hastily, he put his hand up to the tiny hole in the doorway so the gatekeeper beyond could see the Dusk Raven tattoo on his palm.

Severin tapped his foot while he waited for a response from the other side. He'd never been a patient man, so even a moment or two of waiting could make him irate.

What felt like eons later, he finally heard scraping on the other side of the door, then the sound of a handle twisting and the door opening inward.

"Finally," he growled.

He peered into the dimly lit room beyond. A young initiate's eyes stared blankly back at him.

Curious, Severin thought. Where was Daniel? Daniel was the Master's most trusted assistant. He was always there to greet people at the doorway, but not today.

Wondering if this was a sign of bad things to come and with no way to know for sure, it made him uneasy.

Severin waved his hands dismissively at the initiate. "Just lead me onward already, you moron!"

The initiate scraped and bowed deeply, then gestured with one hand for Severin to follow him.

Severin nodded and stepped fully into the room, allowing his grotesque features to come into view of the initiate.

To put it bluntly, he looked hideous. One of his eyes was missing from a scuffle several years back, and a massive scar took its place. The other side of his face bore the marks of a recent fire. It gave the impression that his skin had started to melt off his skull, and his lips had pulled back in one spot in a permanent snarl.

The young initiate, to his credit, said nothing, not even a twitch or slight shudder at the disfigurement.

He's trained them better than I thought, Severin mused. He'd expected the young lad to recoil in horror.

Maybe the horrors they experienced here were far worse. Severin decided he didn't intend to stick around long enough to find out.

He had his people to go back to, and they were counting on him to help rebuild. That was far more important than anything that would happen here.

The young boy led him through a dizzying series of underground tunnels. Severin tried to keep track but soon got lost.

The Dusk Raven stronghold was a veritable underground rat's nest. It was a good tactic, to be sure. If anyone managed to make it to their front door, they would still lose precious time trying to find their way around in the dark. Not that anyone ever did, of course.

Severin laughed to himself and kept going. He was lost in the array of mismatched hallways, but he knew it was the point, so he paid it no heed. He'd be at his destination soon enough.

A moment later the initiate stopped in his tracks and wordlessly motioned to an old stone door in front of them.

It was closed and nondescript, like all the doors in this place, but that meant nothing. He was here. The place where the meeting of generals was to take place.

For a moment, he thought about knocking, then decided against it. Better not make a scene in the Master's presence.

Instead, Severin walked through the door with his head bowed. The Master should appreciate his humility in this instance.

The room that awaited him was well-lit, which was unusual. The Master typically preferred his meetings in the half-light. It made it easier to hide things, like weapons in case the meeting didn't go as planned.

He took in the whole room at once. There was only one person in the room at the moment, a small girl.

Not the one who'd caused him so much trouble. She looked to be in her mid-twenties and semi-attractive in a homely sort of way. She was a bit on the tall side for a girl with shoulder-length brown hair and dark gray eyes.

In any other circumstance, Severin would have been tempted to do awful things to her in the name of the Dusk Ravens, but now was neither the time nor place. He tried to place her. She wasn't familiar, and he was pretty sure he knew all of the Master's generals.

The council hadn't started yet, so he walked up beside the young girl and snorted to make his presence known.

The girl looked at him briefly, then went back to staring at the wall.

"Not much of a conversationalist, eh?" he quipped in a gravelly voice.

The young thing shook her head ever so slightly and remained silent.

Severin was impressed. The girl didn't seem the least bothered by his appearance or gruff demeanor. He expected no less from a general of the Master, even if he didn't know her.

He tried to speak to her a couple more times, but she remained tight-lipped. She was harder to crack than an oyster with bare hands. It started to annoy him.

Not to mention, there was no one else there. The Master had been adamant about the time of the meeting. It wasn't like the Master to be late to anything. He was always the first one there.

Something was definitely amiss. Severin didn't know what it was, but something about the whole situation was off like it was a trap or a trial of some kind.

Severin snorted again and huffed. "Looks like the Master is a no-show to his own event, eh?" he said to no one in particular.

The girl next to him shrugged.

Severin scowled in response. He was about done. He had better things to do with his time than stand around playing whatever game the Master was playing with him.

"I don't have time for this crap," he snorted. "I have a base to run. Tell the Master I'm sorry I missed him, sweet cheeks."

He smacked the young girl on the ass once for good measure and turned away to head for the door.

"Leaving so soon?" a voice called from behind him.

The hair on Severin's neck stood on end. That was the Master's voice. He was sure of it, and it was coming from the same direction as the young girl.

He turned to face the little bitch. She was smiling at him with a dark, evil grin.

"Come on, after all that foreplay the least you could do is finish the job," the Master's voice said from those sweet-looking lips.

Severin blushed. At least that's what he imagined he did. He wasn't sure if he had enough living skin left on his face to pull it off.

He'd heard that the Master could change his appearance at will, but had yet to see it in action himself. Which meant he'd just made a fool of himself in front of the Master by smacking the man square on his ass.

Severin bowed once hastily. "My apologies, Master," he said through clenched teeth. "I didn't know-"

"That it was me?" the Master finished. "Neither did anyone else. That was the point of the test."

The Master made a broad-sweeping motion with his hands. All around the room, one by one, the remaining generals of the Dusk Ravens became visible. The Master had hidden them all from view.

Some of them were snickering at him.

His sense of unease deepened. It hadn't been the Master

that he'd embarrassed himself in front of, but rather the whole damn crew. He'd be lucky to make it out alive today.

"Though I must say, you're the only one that had the balls to smack my ass," the Master continued. "I could get used to that kind of initiative."

In spite of himself, Severin managed half a smile. Maybe he wasn't in as much trouble as he thought. His brash actions could have gained him favor.

The Master motioned for Severin to take a spot next to the other generals. Severin quickly obeyed. He'd won the moment but had no desire to press his luck.

Once he'd taken his spot, the Master uttered something unintelligible and his appearance started to shimmer. A moment later, a giant of a man had taken the place of the small girl. This man had stark black hair that stuck out at odd angles and a full beard. His left ear had a massive piece of metal sticking out of the earlobe and he was wearing a loincloth.

Severin shuddered ever so slightly. This look was no better than the last, and a lot less easy on the eyes. Fortunately, the Master seemed not to notice his distaste.

"That's better," the Master said to the assembled generals. "Now, who knows why I've brought you all here today?"

Silence greeted him. It seemed no one knew the answer. At the very least, no one was willing to chance giving the wrong one. The second option was far more likely.

At long last, Severin spoke. "We're here to talk about that stupid girl."

The Master nodded at him. "Yes, dearie. We are here to

talk about the girl. Though I'd not be so quick as to label her stupid. She outsmarted you once already."

Severin grunted and waved his hand in a dismissive gesture. "She got the drop on me. On equal footing, she wouldn't stand a chance with any of us."

His words were greeted by several nods and a couple of snorts by the other assembled generals.

"Tsk tsk," the Master replied, wagging a finger in his face. "I wouldn't be so sure, Severin. This stupid girl of yours managed to get the better of my top assassin Lucien without the benefit of surprise on her side."

Severin gasped. Lucien was dead? He quickly scanned the room. The little man wasn't among the faces in the assembly.

He'd never really cared for Lucien on a personal level - all that skulking about was unbecoming of a real man - but he couldn't doubt the man's skill with a blade, and the bitch had bested him on equal footing. Severin didn't know how that was even possible

Severin shook his head. "I can't believe it, sir. The girl must have had some sort of help."

The Master dipped his head. He placed one of his massive hands on Severin's shoulder blade and pressed downward ever so slightly. The pressure of that hand was quite intense and Severin had to strain to keep from bending.

"I agree with you, Severin. She must have had help. It's the only thing that makes any sense."

"Pfft. Utter nonsense," a voice called out from the far side of the room. Severin looked toward the voice's source.

It was Zachariah, a tall, dark-skinned man from the southern regions.

Severin had always admired Zachariah. He was like himself in many respects, a man who used muscle and steel to solve his problems and not weird magic stuff. He'd like to get to know Zachariah better one of these days, given a chance.

"Lucien was a half-wit, always relying on magic instead of steel and sense. My pinky finger could have felled him given half the chance," Zachariah finished. He wagged his pinky in the air in a dainty gesture to accentuate his point.

"A half-wit, you say?" The Master craned his neck to look down at Zachariah.

The general nodded once and spit on the ground. "I could have ground the poor sop under my boot. Would have, too, given half a reason."

"Indeed, you might have, Zachariah. But this girl we're talking about is a different matter. She is not big and strong like you. She's from a backwater town in the middle of nowhere. A girl like that shouldn't have the resources she does."

Zachariah eyed the Master and nodded slowly. "Aye, I suppose you're right."

The Master shot him a fierce glare.

"Master," Zachariah added under his breath.

The Master flashed his teeth at the general. "That's better. It wouldn't do to forget your place. Or the one who put you there."

Zachariah bowed his head. A few of the other generals snickered at him until the Master called for silence with a wave of his hand.

"I will have decorum in my presence, or you will all suffer the consequences," the Master hissed. "Make no mistake. All of you can be replaced. There are many that would like the chance."

The Master looked around the room, locking eyes with each general to make sure they got his point loud and clear. The room was far quieter after that.

"That's much better," the Master said, his lips curling into a smile. "Now, as I was saying, what does this stupid little girl have that others like her do not? We must know, lest we all suffer a similar fate to poor Lucien."

A room full of somber nods was all that greeted him.

The Master cleared his throat. "I said, does anyone have any ideas? Pray none of you let me down again."

It appeared the Master had made his point clear as the room erupted into noise a moment later. Everyone was shouting off one idea or another about what they'd like to do to the girl in question, given a chance. The Master let it go for a moment before calling for silence again.

"I appreciate your zeal, children, really I do," the Master told them. "But none of your plans gets us closer to an answer and it's answers I want."

All of the generals bowed their heads in shame, unable to even look at each other. At length, one of the generals, Robert by name, broke the uneasy silence. "We need a recon mission," he suggested in a hushed tone.

"What was that?" the Master asked. Robert repeated his statement, louder and more certain this time.

The Master nodded. "Yes, indeed. Reconnaissance. We need to know everything about this girl. Her name. Her age. Her home life. Her boyfriend if she has one. We must know it all." He grinned even broader. "And then we must take it from her."

Wicked smiles greeted the Master from every corner of the room as eyes lit up with the thought of new evils that could be performed.

"Severin," the Master called.

"Yes, Master?" Severin picked his head up to stare into the Master's eyes.

"I'd like you to head up this effort. You've run into this girl before, so you may already have some leads."

"Me?" Severin replied in a startled tone. "You want me to do recon?"

Inwardly, he was scowling again, though he dare not show it. The last thing he wanted was to go on some B.S. fact-finding mission. He needed to be out in the field with his men, helping them rebuild. Who would help his men if he was stuck off in some backwater town?

He knew better than to deny a request from the Master, so he didn't show even a hint of displeasure.

"Yes, Master," he agreed slowly with a slight bow.

He wondered if this was a punishment for his earlier failure to stop her in the camp. There were other generals that were better equipped to do recon than him.

"Good. Take your full contingent of men that are still at the Dusk Raven camp outside Stratton and go to Chatwick. Find out what you can about the girl, then do what you want with the place."

Severin smiled. Terrorizing the populace? Now that was something he could get behind. "With pleasure."

"Chatwick?" a voice called out from near the back of the room. The voice's owner took a few steps forward. It was Humboldt, a general in charge of most of the Alpen-wood. "That's my area!" he whined. "You'll ruin my long-standing operation if you send someone else in there now!"

"Tsk, tsk, tsk." The Master shook his head slowly at Humboldt. "Are you doubting my orders?"

Humboldt lowered his head. "No, Master," he said in a defeated tone.

Severin snorted. That little snot-nosed general folded like a girl's fan. No wonder he was in charge of backwater towns.

"Besides," the Master continued. "If you were running your operation well enough, I wouldn't have had to send in someone else, now would I?"

Humboldt backed up even further and Severin let out the slightest chuckle. Way to put that dolt in his place.

"I assure you, your long-standing operation will be just fine, Humboldt. This is a recon operation, not a takeover," the Master told him. "I still have need of your special talents there."

That seemed to satisfy the man. He gave a slight bob of his head and slinked back into his corner.

The Master looked amongst the gathered generals. "Now, is there any other business to discuss?" he asked.

A few voices spoke up about various details - arms shipments that needed delivery, changes to camp numbers and makeup, and the like, but Severin wasn't listening to any of it. He had a new mission to undertake, one he was very much starting to like.

Several hours later, the conference was over, and the room started to clear. Severin said his goodbyes to the generals, including Zachariah, and bade goodbye to the Master. Then he turned and left himself.

In his mind he was contemplating his new mission. He didn't know what kind of place Chatwick was, but it would soon be his to command. Humboldt be damned. Recon mission be damned. It was time to play the game his way.

He was going to enjoy playing with that little bitch from Chatwick. It was enough to make him smile.

Several hours later on the same day it was starting to get dark outside the Dusk Raven base, and even the Master's own chambers were returning to the more natural half-light he liked.

Darkness was preferable most of the time, save for during his magical experiments. Those required bright light. A smile came to the Master's lips. He did so love his experiments. If only they would bear more fruit. But alas, his current quest for knowledge seemed to continually elude his grasp.

The Master paced about the room and focused on his next appointment. This meeting would be far different from the previous one. Only one person was expected, his current student.

It wasn't often he took a student on directly. He had trained others in the art of magic long ago so they could do it for him, but every now and then a particularly promising soul came around and he couldn't resist. His current student was one of those people.

A few moments later, four short knocks came at the

door to his chamber. It was unusual for people to knock, but not unheard of.

The Master took a moment to decide on an appearance that was appropriate. He finally settled on an olive-skinned man of average height and appearance. There was no need to confuse or dominate in this upcoming meeting, so he could go with something more natural.

"Come in," the Master said to the person on the other side of the door. His words were greeted by the sound of the door creaking open.

An unfortunate side-effect of having a complex like this deep underground was that everything stayed just a little damp, so even newer doorways creaked as the moisture warped the wood in the frames. Still, it was a small complaint about an otherwise flawless design.

A hooded figure strode through the door, head pointed down to keep from showing his face. Of course, the Master knew who it was, but he was willing to let his student keep up his little farce. It made the other man feel better to pretend everything was still a secret. It was a harmless illusion.

The Master smiled at the younger man. "Ah, how good to see you, my student. Please, do make yourself comfortable."

The hooded figure nodded and moved about silently until he was in the center of the room, then stopped. His head never lifted once.

"So tell me, young one. Any news of the outside to bring to me?"

The hooded man bobbed his head. "A little. I learned

the identity of your mystery woman while I was out. She goes by the name Sariah."

The Master rubbed his chin thoughtfully. "Sariah, you say?" The hooded man nodded. "The name sounds familiar somehow. I should know it from somewhere."

"I've learned a few other things about her as well. She has magic ability. Someone has been training her."

The Master cocked his head to the side in surprise. "Magic training, you say? But from whom? This would have been good information to have earlier." He chuckled. "I know at least one person who would have liked to know."

He shrugged his shoulders. "No matter. I'm sure the fool will find out on his own soon enough. He's got enough guards with him it should make precious little difference in the long run."

The hooded man laughed. "If you say so, Master."

The Master eyed him coolly. His student seemed off today, though exactly how he wasn't sure.

Maybe the air was still stale from the earlier meeting.

"Surely, that's not all you've learned while you were out there in the world by yourself, dearie?" the Master asked at length.

The hooded man shook his head. "No Master, it's not. I've so much more information to share with you. But first..."

"Yes?" the Master replied. "Well, what is it?"

The hooded man took a half a step forward and lowered his voice. "How go the experiments, Master? Have you made any breakthroughs?"

The Master chuckled. "That is why you are my student,

child. You crave power above all else, much like me." His expression soured. "Sadly, no, I have not, though I feel I'm on the cusp of a breakthrough. Worry not, you will be the first to know the moment things change. Provided you continue to keep up your end of the bargain, that is."

"Yes, Master. Of course."

Another smile crossed the Master's lips. "Now, child, where were we? Ah yes. Tell me what you've learned of the world since we met last. Leave no detail out. Even the slightest thing may end up being of the greatest importance."

"Of course, Master," his apprentice replied. Then he sat on the ground and motioned for the Master to do the same.

The Master readily complied. It was going to be a long night. He could sense it already. Long but rewarding.

CHAPTER SEVEN

Harvey took a deep breath to try and help calm his nerves. It was only semi-successful.

With one hand, he reached up and wiped a bead of sweat off his brow. That bead of sweat had been angling precariously toward his eyes, which would have spelled certain doom for him.

His gaze darted around. There was nothing but plains and trees as far as he could see. Wherever his quarry was, they were well hidden.

Not a moment later, he heard the distinct sound of an arrow rushing past his head, missing him by mere inches.

Instinctively, he ducked low to the ground to make himself a harder target in case the attack would be followed by another, but nothing more came.

Harvey looked around again, squinting against the sharpness of the morning light overhead.

I'm a sitting duck out here all alone like this, he thought darkly. He needed to find cover before he became a pincushion.

Up ahead, he spotted a small copse of trees not too far away. It was in the opposite direction than the earlier arrow had come from. Those trees would afford him momentary cover and the chance to think. It would be risky making a break for them, but worth it.

Just then he heard another arrow whizz past him. This one was even closer than the last.

That made up his mind for him. He took a quick look around, then got up and sprinted for the trees as fast as he could.

He heard another couple of arrows plunk into the ground as he ran. Each time he dodged to the side, hoping the last-minute movements would keep him safe. It worked.

A few more giant strides and he was there. Hastily, he ducked behind one of the massive tree trunks. Its bulk should hide him from the assailant well enough.

Harvey took a few deep breaths to slow his heart rate. He needed to think clearly and focus if he was going to make it out of this alive.

Where is that damn archer? he wondered.

It was hard enough facing an opponent you could see. He didn't know what he was supposed to do about one he couldn't.

He shook his head to clear his thoughts. This line of thinking wasn't going to help him see another sun-up. He needed a plan.

As he sat there, he heard another two arrows thunk into the tree behind him. The archer seemed to have a rather large quiver at his disposal. Harvey thought maybe he was almost out, but a few thunks later, he debunked that theory.

He took a glance over his shoulder back toward the direction of the arrows. He still couldn't see anyone, but with the sun in its current position, there could be a whole army at the top of that hill, and he'd be none the wiser.

A realization dawned on him. He pulled on his face and stood up. There was nothing for it. He'd have to try and charge the assailant, fireballs blazing. There was no other option.

He cracked his neck a couple times and gave his legs a quick stretch. He'd really have to sprint and didn't want to get a sudden cramp that would slow him down and spell his doom.

Harvey turned and left the cover of the trees. He growled fiercely at his opponent on top of the hill, a growl that would set any foe on edge.

Then he ran for it. He shot forward as fast as he could, hoping to catch the assailant off-guard.

In his right hand, he charged a fireball, ready to fling it at the first thing he saw.

After a short sprint, he reached the top of the hill to find...nothing.

"Come on!" he moaned. "How is there no one here! Come out of hiding, damn you!"

There was, of course, no answer.

It was worse than he thought. He wasn't facing a hard to find archer, but an invisible one. That lowered his odds of success considerably.

A second later, he heard the sound of another arrow rush past his ear. Quickly, he turned and thrust his fireball in the direction the arrow had come. It impacted a small stump behind him and set it immediately ablaze.

"Damn it!" he swore. That wasn't what he'd wanted to happen. He summoned forth a thin sheet of ice and placed it over the fire to help put it out. The flames would only add to his distractions, the last thing he needed.

He felt another bead of sweat forming on his brow and hastily wiped it away. If he wasn't careful, he'd go blind before he found his attacker. Which, he thought darkly, would mean he had the same chance of finding them as he did now.

The thought made him chuckle in spite of the direness of his situation.

He didn't have long to focus on that thought, either, for not a moment later he heard a low growl come from behind him. The hair on the back of his neck stood on edge.

As hesitant as he was to take a glance, he knew he had no real choice.

A quick peek over his shoulder told him all he needed to know. Behind him stood a massive creature with thick, black skin and long, sharp claws. The thing easily took up half the hilltop by itself. Its head was a mass of scales and fangs unlike anything he'd ever seen before. A long string of saliva dripped from a corner of its mouth onto the ground below it. The creature also had an equally grue-some-looking tail that promised to wreak havoc on him.

"Scheisse!" he shouted. He backed up a half a step invol-untarily and felt himself come into contact with the remains of the tree stump he'd set ablaze moments earlier.

He stumbled backward and tried to remain upright but

was unsuccessful and ended up sprawling onto the ground and losing his weapon in the process.

A stream of expletives left his lips as he turned over and got back to his feet. He held up his hand only to realize that his sword lay about five feet away from him, at the base of the giant creature.

The beast opened its giant maw and howled. The sound was deafening and the force of it almost sent Harvey sprawling, but he managed to hold his ground.

Thinking fast, he used his magic to make his sword float back into his hand. Now at least he was armed and had some sort of defense.

He brandished his weapon and made a few broad swipes in front of the creature, hoping to scare it away, but the creature stood its ground.

Harvey gulped down the knot of fear forming in his throat and redoubled his attack. He lunged forward and tried to sink his blade into one of the creature's glowing eyes, but it seemed to pass right through it like it wasn't even there.

The creature laughed in a deep, demonic tone. It took a swing at him with one of its massive claws.

Harvey put up his hand to shield himself instinctively and waited for the sting of the creature's claws to rip into his unprotected flesh, but the fated blow never came.

A moment later, the creature, the hilltop, and even the copse of trees in the distance all faded from view.

"You lose," a voice said from over his shoulder. It was Sariah's voice.

Harvey slowly turned and stared at her. She was grinning at him like an idiot. He gave her a playful shove with his empty hand. "A dragon? What the hell was that all about?"

Sariah shrugged and pointed at Bear. "It was all his idea."

Bear, who was standing in front of him panting and holding out his paw like he deserved a treat, gave him a sharp bark like he agreed.

Harvey stared at the animal in disbelief. "You were playing the part of the dragon?" he said. He knelt and scratched Bear's head. "You were a good dragon, yes you were."

The dog ate up the attention. He barked a few more times and licked Harvey's palm.

"I wasn't expecting to face down a fearsome dragon," Harvey whined to no one in particular.

Sariah smirked at him. "Yeah, well you still lost and I won. So pay up."

Harvey groaned, but he had to admit she was right. He motioned for Sariah to turn around and she readily complied. Then he took the gloves off his hands and started scratching her back in all the hard to reach places.

Sariah gave him a slight moan of contentment as his hands moved deftly up and down her spine. "Ooh, that feels so good," she told him. "A bit to the left, please."

Harvey shifted his scratching around, trying to find the spot she wanted.

"Yes, that's the spot," Sariah said a moment later. He felt her body start to lose its tension. "Right there. A little harder."

Harvey kept it up for another few seconds, then he

dropped his hands. "There. You should be good for a while."

Sariah turned to face him again. "Thank you. You give the best back scratches, you know."

Harvey rolled his eyes. "Yeah, yeah. I know. Best scratches in the world." Sariah nodded at him. "You know, we don't have to do all this. You could just ask me."

She laughed. "Yeah, but it's so much more fun this way, don't you think?" She put her hands on her hips. "Especially when you lose."

He shoved her playfully. "Yeah, well you cheated."

"Cheated?" Her face turned into a frown and her eyes widened. "How?"

Harvey pointed toward Bear. "The dragon? That wasn't part of the arrangement."

She gave him a sheepish grin. "Well, technically you never said I couldn't conjure one."

He growled at her, but she was right. Their rules were lax.

Harvey took another look at his surroundings. They looked nothing like they did previously. The tree stump he'd set aflame and tripped over was an old chair now definitely not fit for use any time soon. The copse of trees from before was a line of heavy boxes that contained who knows what.

They were in the basement of The Dragonfly. After their little scuffle with the Dusk Raven bandits the other day, the two of them had agreed to confine their training to inside the inn in order to stay out of trouble. Their cramped little rooms didn't give a lot of space for in-depth training in magic and were woefully inadequate for weapons training, and they still needed heaps of both.

It had been Sariah's idea to talk to Evelyn, the innkeeper of The Dragonfly. She seemed to get along with their middle-aged caretaker for some reason. He thought about asking Sariah about it sometime, but could never come up with the right words to say. That was often a problem for him around Sariah.

After a little pressing, Evelyn let on the inn had a large basement that had gone unused for some time and she would be only too happy to let the two of them use it for their own thing, so long as neither of them made a mess of things down there.

They'd done their best to keep up with their side of the bargain, this morning's little chair fire notwithstanding. He looked down at the old, broken chair now beyond repair and flashed it one of his dopey grins.

Inwardly, he hoped he wouldn't have to explain this to Evelyn. Maybe he could hide its broken remains under the blanket in the far corner with the other discarded pieces. It was as good a plan as any.

It had been Sariah's idea to enhance the space with her mental magic and make it look like an actual battleground.

She was able to use magic to make their surroundings look like anything she wanted, and as Harvey had noted today, also add in visual and audio hallucinations to make the experience all the more real.

He only wished he could return the favor, but even the most basic mental magic spells seemed to elude his grasp. He reaped all the rewards while Sariah did all the hard work. Still, she seemed only too happy to do it, and the exercise was really pushing him to his outer limits, which would only help in the long run.

Harvey looked at Sariah. She was still smirking at him like an idiot, obviously quite pleased with her performance.

Truth be told, the Bear-turned-dragon bit had been a nice touch, even if it had scared him half to death. Not that he'd ever admit it.

Harvey returned Sariah's smile with a big, dopey grin of his own.

"Ready to go another round?" he asked her.

Sariah nodded firmly. "You know it. Only this time I won't hold back as much."

He looked down at the sword in his hand and then up at her. "Bring it on."

Harvey liked this, he decided, getting to spend time alone with Sariah while working toward a common goal. He could get used to it. He only hoped she liked it just as much as he did.

***

Gabe huffed and walked through the streets of Stratton as fast as his tired feet could carry him. He'd spent a lot of energy earlier in the day teleporting from one point to another and he was tired.

All he wanted at the moment was a hot bath and a rest, but he knew he wouldn't be that lucky. He had information Sariah would want the moment he returned. He knew if he kept it secret till morning, he would end up paying the price later. He'd waited long enough as it was since he was already returning several days later than he'd originally planned.

He sighed. It was all part of being a team player, he supposed. Inwardly, he groaned and wondered if he had made the right decision taking on apprentices and becoming part of a team the way he had.

It was no use wondering about it now. The past was in the past. He'd made his decision, and there was no easy way to go back on it. Besides, both Sariah and Harvey were starting to grow on him. He could get used to this whole having companions to watch his back thing.

It was comforting in a way.

He rounded another bend and The Dragonfly came into view. He was almost there and back to safety.

Maybe he'd be lucky and Sariah would let him rest for the night. He shook his head. Sariah was impulsive. She'd demand they leave right away.

Oh well, he sighed. It was all for the best.

He strode up to the doors of The Dragonfly and opened them slowly. The smell of acrid weed smoke and the harsh light of candles greeted him. There were a couple of people in the common area eating what looked to be some kind of stew.

Gabe stepped inside and placed his back against the wall. He let himself take it all in - the sights and sounds of happy people. It was quite different from where he'd spent the better part of the last week.

He shuddered remembering. They weren't fond memories. Necessary, perhaps, but not good. Not like the time he spent with Sariah.

Gabe took another few moments to bask in the warmth

of the room, then he nodded once to Evelyn and wandered upstairs.

As he walked, he started to wonder what his little apprentices had gotten up to while he was gone and if they were still in one piece even.

They must be, he decided, or Evelyn would have stopped him and said something. He could count on her to be a good caretaker for the two and keep them out of trouble for the most part.

He had a long-shared history with Evelyn, that traced back to before his days with the Dusk Ravens. It's why he'd picked this place originally. He knew he could count on her to keep all his secrets, even this one.

Gabe stopped outside the door to Sariah and Harvey's room. He brought up one hand to knock, then dropped it. He wasn't quite ready to go in yet, he decided. He needed one more moment to rest and catch his breath before stepping into all the excitement that waited for him on the other side of the door.

He placed his ear gingerly on the door and tried to listen in on any conversation that might be taking place. In spite of everything, he still doubted their sincerity.

And why not? he mused. It wasn't like he was completely truthful with them, either.

He strained his ears for a few moments, but there was nothing. He wondered if they were sleeping, but doubted it. It was still the dinner hour downstairs. It wasn't like his students to be asleep at this hour. As young as they were, they could stay up half the night training sometimes and still manage to be bright-eyed the next morning.

He'd spent enough time stalling. It was time to announce his presence

He thought about knocking once more but decided against it. His little knocking ritual was a tad silly. Instead, he slowly turned the doorknob and opened the door, then walked inside.

What awaited him in the room beyond brought a tear to his eye. Both of his apprentices sat with piles of stones in front of them. They were manipulating the rocks into a complicated pattern in the air with their minds.

The stones made the vague outline of an animal's head. Bear's, maybe. It was hard to tell for sure with just an outline.

Speaking of the dog, he was off in the corner snoozing away, happy as could be.

Gabe smiled and looked over his two students with pride. They'd taken his advice to heart and were finally training like they were supposed to be.

Sariah caught sight of him out of the corner of one of her coal-black eyes. She blinked a couple times and her eyes returned to their normal color.

"Gabe!" she squealed. She ran over to him and gave him a big hug, which he readily accepted. In the meantime, her half of the stones clattered onto the ground, forgotten.

"It's good to see you, too," he replied. He let himself enjoy her hug for a moment longer. The feel of her skin up close against him was warming and welcoming in a way he hadn't expected. He pushed her away slightly without letting go completely.

"Hey, Sariah, what's going on? Why'd you drop your

stones? The portrait was almost done!" Harvey's voice called out from across the room.

The kid blinked a few times as well then finally looked around and noticed Gabe and Sariah standing there, still half in an embrace. A flash of anger or maybe deep embarrassment crossed his cheeks and was gone just as quickly.

"Gabe. Nice to see you back so soon," Harvey said coolly. His greeting wasn't nearly as warm as Sariah's had been. Not that he should expect as much, of course.

Sariah let go of him and turned to face Harvey. She had a rosy glow to her cheeks. Was she embarrassed as well? It was so hard to tell. He wasn't well versed in human interactions.

"Now, now. Be nice to Gabriel," Sariah chided Harvey, wagging a finger at him. "He's obviously come a long way and is quite tired." She turned to face him. "Isn't that right, Gabe?"

Gabe nodded once. "It's true. I teleported most of the way here to save time. I'm exhausted." He yawned as if to accentuate the point.

Harvey gave him a dopey grin. He lowered his gaze. "Sorry, you're right. I was a little lost in concentration is all," he admitted.

Gabe doubted that was really the case, but there was no point in arguing and he let the point slide.

Sariah walked over to one of the beds and sat down, then patted the bed next to her, motioning for Gabe to take a seat. "Come sit. You must be really tired to have come all that way so fast."

Gabe couldn't believe how nice Sariah was being to him. It wasn't like her.

Does she know what I've really been up to? he wondered. There was no way she'd be this calm if she knew the truth.

She could be trying to hide something, though what that could be, there was no way of telling. Sariah was getting quite good at blocking her mind off from his spells.

There was no use worrying about it for the moment, he thought with a shrug.

He did her bidding and sat next to the girl. It still felt remarkably good to be as close to her as he was. Almost too good. He'd have to watch how close he was getting to her. One should never get too close.

"So," Sariah started. "How was the trip? Tell us all about it."

Gabe stared back at her. She was looking up at him with great, big doe eyes expectantly. It brought a slight smile to his lips.

He sighed once and smoothed out the fabric of his shirt. Then he looked at Harvey, who was standing in the corner and still seemed perturbed but was otherwise fine. He shook his head.

"Uh, the trip was good. Really good," he said at last. He allowed himself to sigh again. "Got everything done that I'd hoped to accomplish, at least."

Sariah rolled her eyes at him. "Oh come on. You know that's not going to cut it. Spill. What happened out there? I want to hear all of it."

Gabe groaned. He had no desire to relive the past few days of dark times. Especially not right now, with Sariah sitting close to him.

"Oh, you know. I met people. Did some stuff. Gathered

new information. That sort of thing. It was quite boring, really." He cleared his throat. "How about you two? What did you get up to while I was gone?"

Sariah shrugged her shoulders. "Oh you know, training and stuff. Nothing exciting. Just staring at boring old rocks all day." She pointed half-heartedly at the rock pile in the center of the room.

Her eyes were shining brightly in the dim light with excitement or a secret, but what it was he couldn't puzzle out. She was a remarkably hard nut to crack when she wanted to be.

"I see," Gabe replied. He slapped his thighs and stood up. "Well, it's been a long few days for everyone it seems. Let's get some shut eye, shall we?" He rubbed his eyes for good measure.

Sariah shook her head. "You really think I'm going to let you off that easy? You've spent over a week out in the world doing who knows what while we've been cooped up in a little inn room the whole time." Her cheeks seemed to redden for just a moment as she said the last sentence, then it was gone. "I need to know what's going on! What's new with the Dusk Ravens, that sort of thing. Spill!"

Gabe blinked. Something must have happened to the two of them while he was gone. He was sure of it now. Sariah was being way too dodgy.

He'd have to wait to get his answers. He could press Harvey about it later and read the kid's thoughts. That kid had no idea how to shield them properly.

He looked at Sariah again. She was still looking at him every bit as expectantly as before. He sighed. There was no getting out of it. He'd have to give his new information here and now.

"The Dusk Ravens, you say?" he started hesitantly. He wiped a small bead of sweat from his brow and looked away. "Oh, not much. Nothing really going on there for the most part."

Sariah scowled. "Really? You're going to have to do better than that."

He sighed again. "You're right, you're right. There is something. It's not much. Just a small rumor I heard on the way in. A trifle of a thing, really." He paused, but Sariah's gaze told him she wouldn't relent.

"You must understand, there's no way to know if it's substantial or not. It could be complete nonsense. I'm warning you about that right now."

Sariah nudged him. She was sitting up straight. "Go on."

Gabe looked down at his feet. He really didn't want to repeat this part. "Well, you see. I um ...I heard the remaining bandits outside Stratton were on the move, actually."

"Yeah?" Harvey chimed in.

Gabe did a double take. It seemed even the kid was interested in what he had to say. "Yeah," he continued. "I heard the whole operation has picked up and is moving, um ...south."

Sariah cocked her head to the side. "South?" She wrinkled her nose and her eyes narrowed. "But there's nothing south of here. Nothing but forests and..."

"Chatwick," Gabe finished for her.

Sariah gasped and her eyes grew wide. "You don't think?"

Gabe put out a hand defensively. "There's no way to know for sure. I'm no longer a Dusk Raven, remember? I have a few old contacts but that's it. They could be heading anywhere."

"But they're not heading anywhere, are they?" Sariah stood up and her body tensed. "They're headed to my hometown, aren't they?"

"I suppose yes, it's possible." He looked deep into her eyes and felt a hint of pity wash over him. "Look, I came to tell you as soon as I found out. It's the best I can do."

Sariah started pacing the floor. "We've got to get moving! Tonight!"

Gabe and Harvey both groaned. "Tonight?" Gabe whined. "I'm exhausted, remember? Can't we get at least some sleep first?"

She shook her head and shot him an icy glare. "My hometown is suffering, and you want to sit around sleeping through it?"

Harvey walked over and put a hand on her shoulder. "I get how you feel, Sariah, but he's right, you know."

She turned and scowled at him. "It's your hometown, too, you know. Your dad's still there, and Padron. All our friends are there, and they're in danger!"

Harvey backed up a half step and put out his hands in front of him. "True, but we're not going to make any headway in the dark. We need to wait until morning." He sighed. "I hate to admit it, but Gabe's right on this one."

Sariah looked at both of them, then grimaced and turned. "Men," she uttered under her breath.

She walked over to Bear and scratched his chin. The

animal opened one sleepy eye and looked up at her. "At least I can count on you, can't I Bear?"

Bear gave her a contented growl and went back to sleep.

Sariah threw up her hands in defeat. "Will no one help me out?" she asked, looking up at the ceiling.

"We will, Sariah. But we need to be smart about this," Gabe implored. "We can't just rush in and hope for the best. We need to have a plan." He rubbed his chin. "Look, we'll all leave first thing in the morning, okay? Promise."

Sariah stared at him for a moment, then groaned. "Fine," she hissed. "We'll do it your way since everyone is against me. But we leave at first light!"

Walking over to the door, she threw it open. "I'm going to take Gabe's room tonight. You losers can sleep in here by yourselves and keep each other company in your loser thoughts."

With that, she walked out of the room and slammed the door behind her.

"You think she'll be okay?" Gabe asked Harvey once the door frame stopped shaking.

The kid stared at the door, mouth agape. "Yeah," he said finally with a nod. "She'll be fine. Just needs some time to cool off, is all. By morning she'll be good to go."

Gabe let out a long sigh. "Good. In that case, I'm going to bed."

CHAPTER EIGHT

Harvey woke with a start. Something wasn't right. He had no idea what just yet, but something was definitely off.

With one hand, he rubbed the grime out of his eyes and looked around the room. It was still dark outside, early dawn perhaps. Off in the other corner of the room lay Gabe and Bear, in the same position he'd recalled them being the night before.

He felt a slight twinge in his fingers and looked down at his hand. The hair was standing on end. His senses were definitely on high alert.

In that same instant, he heard the sound of a floorboard creak outside in the hallway, then there was silence once again.

His eyes darted in Gabe's direction. The man was breathing soundly in bed next to his dog. He hadn't seemed to notice anything. Only Harvey had heard the strange noise.

Slowly, he raised himself from his prone position and

started to climb out of the bed. He didn't want to alarm Gabe without reason.

Moving as quietly as he could, he slipped on his shoes and crept across the floor to the doorway. He wasn't sure who had made the noise in the hallway, but just in case it was a bad actor, he didn't want to alert them to his presence.

Once he reached the door, he pressed his ear against the wood, straining to listen for any further noises from the hallway. He thought he caught someone uttering a few hushed words, but he couldn't make out what they were, or even the gender of the person speaking.

Blood rushed to his extremities as his heart started racing. The sound drowned out everything else, so he gave up eavesdropping.

He took a couple breaths to slow down his heart rate so he could think clearly.

We've been safe enough at The Dragonfly for the past several weeks, he mused, rubbing his chin. There's no reason to think any of that would change now.

Still, he had to be certain.

Harvey reached out and turned the door handle, trying his best to make sure not to make any noise in the process, then he opened the door slowly until there was a crack just big enough for him to see through.

He peered through the crack into the dimly lit hallway beyond. There was nothing there. Even the hushed noises from earlier were gone, replaced with an eerie silence.

He knew there had been someone there a second ago, but didn't know where they could have gotten off to.

Harvey opened the door just enough to allow him to

squeeze through. Entering the hallway, he took another look around, but it appeared he was still alone.

A dark thought came to him and the blood drained from his face.

Sariah! What if this mystery person was after Sariah?

It would make sense. Sariah was convinced this "Master" person was after her. Whoever the Master was, he hadn't made a move in weeks. What better time than now?

He bounded over to her room as fast as he could, no longer caring for stealth, and forced the door to her room open. It was foolish, perhaps, but worth the risk.

The room was empty. Harvey looked about for a moment to be sure. The bed looked like someone had slept in it and was still messy like the inhabitant had left in a hurry.

A knot of fear formed in Harvey's throat. Sariah was gone. Had she left on her own, or had someone taken her? He had no way to know the answer for sure, but both were bad news.

He headed back out toward his own room. He entered it quickly this time, making a racket in the process.

In the corner of the room, Gabriel groaned and rubbed his eyes. "Ugh, what's going on out there?" the older man asked.

"Sariah's gone," Harvey answered.

Gabe shot up out of bed and looked around with bleary eyes. "Gone?" he repeated.

Harvey frowned and nodded. "Yep. She's not in her room. I heard some weird noises this morning and thought I'd go check on her. Nothing."

Gabe furrowed his brow. "You don't suppose?"

"She was taken?" He shook his head. "I mean, I'd like to think the answer was no, but I can't say for sure."

Gabe rubbed his chin. "Well, what are you doing lounging about? We have to go after her!"

Harvey nodded. "My thoughts exactly."

Gabe walked over and roused Bear from his slumber. The dog growled but eventually raised his head.

"Hey!" Gabe said, poking his dog. "Sariah's missing! We need to find her!"

That got the animal moving in a hurry. Bear got up and shook his body, then growled at Gabriel as if to say, "Why didn't you mention this sooner?"

Moving as one, the three headed out the door.

When they were in the hallway, Harvey heard the same hushed noises from earlier. This time, they were coming from the common room downstairs.

Harvey raised a finger to his lips and pointed toward Gabe and Bear to ask for silence. They both nodded.

Taking the lead, Harvey crept forward toward the stairwell, with Gabe and Bear close behind him. He went as fast as he could while remaining quiet.

In the meantime, the noise from the common room stopped, and instead they heard the vague sound of a door opening and closing.

That got Harvey's heart racing. He didn't know if the attacker just left with an unconscious Sariah in tow, and there was only one way to find out for sure.

He raced down the steps at breakneck speed, taking them two at a time and barreled through the common room. He didn't even notice Evelyn sitting behind the counter, shaking her head at his foolish antics.

Reaching the door, he threw it open and was greeted by the first rays of sunlight as they crept over the town gates and blasted him straight in the eyes.

Harvey shielded his vision with one hand and blinked to help his eyes adjust to the harsh light, then looked around every which way for Sariah or her assailants.

When his eyes finally regained their focus, he saw Sariah standing and staring at him with her arms crossed. At her feet lay a rather large parcel wrapped in brown paper.

"There you are!" Harvey blurted out. "I was worried about you!"

Sariah frowned and reached forward to give him a big hug. He readily accepted.

"I got up early and thought I'd get started on buying the provisions," she explained. She pulled away and pointed at the package at her feet. "I wasn't about to let Gabe make all our food choices again. Remember last time?"

Grimacing, Harvey thought back to their last trek. Gabe had indeed bought all the rations and they were almost all completely tasteless.

"I suppose you have a point," he admitted, flashing her a dopey grin.

"Hey!" Gabe whined, but Harvey ignored him.

"Still, you scared me. Us, really. We thought something might have happened to you."

"I didn't mean to startle you," Sariah replied. Her cheeks started to flush, and she averted her gaze. "I was only trying to help."

Harvey let out a long sigh. He felt his heartbeat finally start to slow down and the tension in his shoulders faded.

"No, I'm the one that should apologize," he admitted. His mind was still racing with thoughts of what might have been, but she was safe. That's all that mattered.

"It was wrong of me to assume the worst. Still, you could have been seriously hurt, you know. You can't just run off on your own like that. We're a team, remember?"

Sariah looked up at him and nodded. "Right. You're right. Won't happen again. Now, do you want to see the food I bought or not?" She pointed toward the parcel at her feet again.

Harvey's eyes brightened as he remembered the reason for her outing. His stomach started to growl at the thought of breakfast. "Do I ever!"

Sariah got up and stretched. It was her turn to take watch. They'd been traveling for about a week and a half straight now and were getting close to the vicinity of Chatwick once again. The woods around her were starting to look familiar.

In a way it was nice to be this close to home, even if her last memories there were less than pleasant. She thought back on the past several days. They had not been easy on her. Gabe had insisted that she and Harvey keep up their training in both magic and weapons while they traveled.

While she agreed she needed the training, some of it was harder than she'd expected, like invisibility. The spell itself had been easy enough to cast, but Gabe was teaching her to use it as a way to sneak up on and kill her opponents.

That filled her with a sense of unease. Lucien's specialty had been killing with invisibility. If she did the same, was she really all that different from the people she despised?

She shook her head and rubbed her arms to ward off the slight chill in the morning air. Whatever awaited them in Chatwick wouldn't care what she thought and would certainly use it against her. Maybe she was too hard on herself.

Her eyes wandered over to Harvey sleeping peacefully. She smiled briefly. Harvey had gotten into this mess because of her. He'd been content to live the miner's life before she'd insisted on this journey, and now he was in the same peril as everyone else.

She walked over to him and gently rubbed his forehead. Poor Harvey. His life would never be the same again. Assuming he lived, of course.

What did I do to deserve such great friends? She thought. I'll have to pay him back somehow.

Another sigh escaped her lips. She was starting to pick up the habit from Gabe, she was sure of it - and turned her attention back to her surroundings.

The cold morning air was brisk, but nothing stirred in it. Not even the crickets were bothering her too much. It seems even they had gone to bed. It was calm, much like the last several days had been.

A few hours later, the sun greeted her, signaling the end of her watch. She rubbed her shoulders to warm herself and got about the mundane task of waking her companions.

Once everyone was awake and ready to go, they got about their business of moving onward to Chatwick. They mostly marched in silence, no one really quite sure what to say. It was altogether boring. At least the training sessions were exciting.

Around midday, clouds started forming in the sky, and not nice ones, either. Big, nasty clouds that brought the promise of rain with them.

Sariah groaned. She knew Gabe would force them to trudge right through the rainstorm anyway, but she was dreading it. Marching with wet clothes did not sound like fun.

A break in the trees up ahead signaled they'd reached the small stream they had crossed all those weeks ago when first hunting for Gabe's cabin. At the same time, the promised rain started to fall. It came slowly at first, just tiny little drops that did little more than annoy, then it came down much harder.

Rainfall was unusual for this time of year. Especially a heavy rain like this one. Not that the rain clouds seemed to know that fact.

Sure enough, Gabe informed the others they wouldn't slow down "for a little rain," just like she'd thought he would.

Sariah muttered at him behind his back as she felt her clothes start to stick to her skin. Who'd made him the leader of their hike anyway?

A few minutes later, a miracle happened, and Gabe called for a sudden halt. He put his hand out to the side. "Quiet, everyone," he urged in a hushed tone.

Sariah rolled her eyes at him. "What now?"

For a moment, Gabe said nothing, and just stood with his arm sticking out and rain falling all around him. The older man turned to look at her. "Sorry, I thought I heard something is all. Let's keep going."

She nodded. "Sure thing, boss."

The four of them started marching again. Then, Sariah caught wind of the sound that had freaked Gabe out earlier. It sounded almost like a howl or a low-pitched whine of an animal, but not quite. It was hard to make out since it was coming from far away.

Gabe stopped walking again to listen.

"Is that?" Sariah started.

"An animal?" Gabe replied. He rubbed his chin. "It could be. Hard to be sure."

The sound came again. It was a little closer and definitely sounded like a wolf howl this time.

Gabe put his hand out once more to tell everyone to stop. They complied. "That's an animal, all right. But it doesn't sound like one that belongs around here." His eyes darted around every which way. "Come, let's keep going, but take it slow."

Harvey and Sariah both nodded. Even Bear inclined his head.

They made it another hundred meters perhaps when the noise came again, even closer to their current position and more urgent. There was something else, too. The sound of a human scream, perhaps. It was mangled, and the sound of the rain falling muffled everything, so it was hard to make out.

Gabe took out his sword and held it in his hands. Sariah and Harvey did the same. No one was quite sure what awaited them up ahead, but it was better to be safe than sorry.

They kept going, moving to the sounds. Sariah wondered briefly why they didn't try to head around the sounds to avoid conflict.

Then it came again, even louder than before. There was no mistaking it this time. That was a human scream mixed in among the animal howls. A fellow human was under attack by whatever animal was making that awful racket.

Was it someone from Chatwick? Sariah bit her lip. Probably, which meant one of her people was in danger.

Sariah felt her heart pound in her chest as her protective instincts kicked into high gear. The noises were so loud she was positive the beast and its human victim were just ahead past the next set of trees.

Her hand grabbed the hilt of her sword a little tighter. It was still slick from the rain and she worried it would come loose during the ensuing combat.

The howl came again, breaking through the trees in front of them. It was almost deafening.

Gabe moved first. He darted forward with his weapon held high. Bear was quick on his heels, Sariah and Harvey close behind.

Once they were through the trees, Sariah saw the full scene in front of her at last. In the clearing stood a massive wolf hovering over a human victim. The human looked to be on the older side. It was no one she recognized, at least not initially, though that didn't mean much.

The human had a nasty scar running down his chest and a fresh set of claw marks on his cheek. He looked to be breathing, but from this distance and through the rain, it was hard to be sure.

The massive wolf took most of her attention. It was

easily the largest animal she'd ever seen. She thought it was the same wolf that had attacked them earlier in this area of the woods, all those weeks ago at the start of their quest. It had been darker then and the beast had been hard to make out, but how many giant wolves could there be in this area?

It had to be the same one.

Sariah's lips curled into a mean smile. Payback time, bitch, she thought.

The beast gnashed its teeth and was about to gore its victim when Gabe of all people snarled at the thing, diverting its attention. The wolf turned to look at the new threat and snarled back.

Gabe lunged forward and the wolf dodged quickly to the side. It seemed the beast didn't like four on one odds nearly as much as it liked single combat, which was good news for them.

Sariah let out a battle cry and charged the beast. When she was close, she made a wild swing with her blade but slipped on fresh mud. She missed the beast entirely and went sprawling into the trees beyond it instead.

Not her best move. Fortunately, Gabe, Harvey, and Bear were there to keep its attention, giving her ample time to recover.

She got up and wiped some mud off her shirt, then eyed the situation. The beast looked cornered, with Gabe, Harvey, and Bear all advancing on it slowly from different directions.

That could be good or bad. It was hard to tell exactly what a cornered wolf would do.

Sariah started back in on the beast and in the same

instant, Harvey broke formation and rushed the wolf, blade held out in front.

Harvey was more successful than she had been and managed to get a glancing blow on the animal's side. It howled and recoiled, then lashed out with its massive claw.

She watched as one of the beast's giant paws impacted the side of Harvey's head.

Her heart dropped. It was just like the last encounter all over again!

Sariah was determined to do something about it this time. She eyed the distance to the wolf. It was too great. She'd have to use magic.

She brought her hands together and pulled them apart, forming a mini fireball in between, then she let it loose.

The fireball flew from her hands and went flying right in between the wolf and Gabe, impacting neither of them but sending Gabe flying back to dodge out of the way at the last second. It ran into a tree where it sizzled and died quickly on the soaked wood.

Sariah squeaked. That hadn't been the intended result.

The wolf took advantage of everyone's momentary confusion and made a swipe at Gabe's midsection, which connected. Gabe was forced to the ground.

Sariah frowned. Everything was going wrong. She was only trying to help, but all her efforts were backfiring spectacularly.

While she was planning her next move, the wolf locked eyes with her. It was obvious what the beast intended. It wanted to take her out, too, then make a feast out of all of them.

She looked at the sword at her side, then back up at the

wolf. Would steel succeed where magic had failed her? There was only one way to know.

She wiped her hands off on a dry-ish patch of her shirt and tightened her grip on the sword anew. It was just her and the wolf now.

The wolf lunged at her, but she was ready for it this time. She dodged toward the left and the wolf went sailing past her.

In the process, she tried a back-handed swipe at the creature, but she slipped in the fresh mud again and her blade went wide.

Sariah scowled and shouted at the beast. She would see it dead if it was the last thing she did.

The wolf lunged for her again. This time, she ducked under the massive creature and held her sword aloft like a pike.

It sliced into the creature's neck, leaving a nasty-looking wound that unfortunately didn't seem to be fatal.

Now the wolf was on top of her. She stabbed up at the creature again and made contact, cutting a deep wound into its midsection.

The wolf howled in pain and reared back. Sariah took the momentary break to steady herself and get ready for the next assault.

She managed to get to her knees before the wolf came for her again. She tried to stab it as it advanced once more, but the beast was ready for her and dodged her blade.

Sariah, however, was not so lucky. One of the beast's massive paws struck her in the leg and she fell back to the ground.

She looked at her leg briefly. There were a couple of

fresh red marks there from the beast's claws. They hurt like hell, but she had no time to think about it, for the beast was coming for her again.

Sariah reached for her blade to defend herself, but it wasn't there. She looked about in shock and saw it lying on the ground a few feet away.

Concentrating on the blade, she tried to make it fly into her hand with magic only it disobeyed and didn't budge.

The wolf let out a low growl and bared its fangs. Then it advanced on her.

Sariah said a quick prayer to the Matriarch and waited for the attack.

CHAPTER NINE

Gabe's head hurt, but at least it wasn't bleeding. The wolf's attack had forced him to the ground, where his head had hit a loose stone. There would be a bad bruise there for a couple of days, but it was nothing to write home about.

His stomach, on the other hand, hurt like hell. He clutched it once with his free hand and tried his best to stand.

He didn't have time to give in to the pain. The wolf was still very much alive, and Sariah was attacking it alone. He had to help.

Gabe sat up and a wave of pain rocked his abdomen. He looked down and saw a rather deep gash across his midsection. As bad as it looked, it felt even worse.

He clenched his teeth and fought through the pain. Sariah was more important. He could deal with the scratch later.

With great effort, he stood and blinked a few times to clear the rain out of them, hoping to get a good grasp of the current situation.

Harvey was off to his right. The boy wasn't moving.

That left Sariah and Bear, who were fighting the wolf.

He scanned the clearing. Sariah was standing close to the wolf, sword in hand. She appeared to be unhurt, at least for the time being. Bear, meanwhile, was doing his best to circle around to the back of the beast and not be seen.

Gabe smiled. Good boy, he thought. Bear was doing exactly what he'd trained the dog to do.

Just then, the wolf made a swipe at Sariah that sent the girl sprawling.

Fear for her gripped him and gave him the strength to get moving. He half-stumbled forward while clutching his sword in one hand and his stomach in the other.

For a moment, he considered magic, but in this weather and in such close quarters, he had as much chance of hitting Sariah as he did the wolf. Magic was out. He'd need cold steel.

The wolf raised one of its massive paws like it was about to strike. Gabe's eyes narrowed and he let loose a battle-cry at the top of his lungs. The sound of it seemed to stun the beast for a half a second.

That gave Bear just enough time to finally make his advance. The dog leaped on the wolf from behind, catching one of its hind legs in his jaws.

The massive beast howled and reared about trying to shake Bear loose, but he wouldn't let go.

Gabe smiled at the dog once more. Bear was a worthy companion. He'd have to remember to get the animal some bacon treats later.

He advanced on the wolf, weapon out in front. When he got closer, he noticed splotches of blood on the animal's rain-tattered coat. It seemed Sariah had been at least some-what successful in her battle.

Gabe lunged at the beast's side and thrust his blade forward with all his might. The blade sank in deep. So deep that when the wolf tumbled to the side, it took the blade with him.

He moved forward and looked at the wounded animal. It still had a little fight left in it, but not much.

The beast gnashed its fangs and stared up at Gabe with a look of hatred in its eyes.

Gabe snarled back at it.

The wolf shot up and came at him with one of its massive paws. It seemed the beast wasn't as out of it as he'd thought.

He was caught off-guard and they both careened onto the ground in a tangled mass of limbs and fur.

The beast tried to snap at his face with its massive jaws so Gabe did the only thing he could think of and held its mouth open with both of his hands, trying to force it away.

The beast howled in pain again, and it backed off once more. Bear must have gone in for another attack.

Gabe got to his feet and surveyed the wolf. It had his sword still sticking out of a massive bleeding wound in its side and both of its hind legs were now injured. The thing was limping hard and would likely die soon, but still it pressed the attack.

How odd, he thought. It wasn't like a wolf to attack like this alone. It was no ordinary creature and he pitied the beast more than anything.

A fireball came flying over his head and careened into

the injured side of the wolf. The creature fell, its flesh and fur burning even in the rain.

Gabe looked over his shoulder. Harvey was grinning at him with one of his signature dopey grins.

He wasn't sure if he wanted to yell at the kid for using magic in such close quarters or hug him. In the end, he did neither and just grinned back.

The wolf gave off one last howl, then stopped moving.

A few moments later, the flames on its corpse went out and the rain stopped falling. The grand battle was over.

Gabe took one last look around to make sure Harvey and Sariah both looked safe, then he fell to the ground and everything went black.

Sariah surveyed the damage. She tried to stand on her bad leg. It hurt, but it was manageable. She could live with the pain.

Harvey seemed to have suffered no more than a few scratches and bumps, and Bear, thankfully, was no worse for the wear.

Gabe, on the other hand, looked to be in pretty bad shape, as did the wolf's original victim. Both men had rather large scratches and were currently unconscious. It was just her luck the one person with healing magic was also the one who currently couldn't use it and also needed it the most.

A big sigh escaped her lips. Today really had not been her day.

She looked up at the sky. It was clearing and the sun

was beating down on them once again. At least the weather was looking up.

Sariah called Harvey over. Instead of him standing around looking like an idiot without a clue, she sent him on a mission to try and find some dry wood to build a fire.

Gabe didn't normally allow fires. He said it announced their presence to the world, but right now she really didn't care. She was more worried about Gabe and the mystery person dying if they didn't get help. Warmth was at least a start.

It wasn't much, but it was something she could do.

Meanwhile, she dragged both of their bodies out of the really muddy spots to a spot that was hopefully drier. Again, it was a small thing, but it made her feel better than doing nothing.

Soon enough, Harvey came back with some wood that looked like it would do the job. He set it down in the clearing and cast a fireball to light it ablaze. Then the two of them carefully positioned their patients in front of the flames.

With the immediate threats cleared, Sariah started examining their injuries in earnest.

Remarkably, the mystery man appeared to be in decent shape, even though he'd faced the wolf alone. His wounds looked vicious, but they weren't overly deep and would probably heal on their own over time.

Gabe hadn't been so lucky. The gash in his abdomen was deeper than she liked. Without advanced care, he might not pull through.

She wasn't really sure how to help him out, but she couldn't sit and wait for the inevitable, so she settled on making bandages out of a spare shirt. At least maybe she could stem some of the bleeding.

As she started tearing apart a spare shirt, Harvey came over.

"That looks pretty bad," he said, pointing to Gabe's wounds.

Sariah nodded. "Why do you think I'm making bandages, genius?"

Harvey backed off and held up his hands in defense.

Sariah scowled at herself. She'd been harsher on him than he deserved, especially considering he was the one who'd put the wolf out of its misery and saved them all.

All she'd done was mess things up and make them worse. She couldn't even direct a fireball properly, and it had petered out way faster than Harvey's had.

Harvey's fireball had worked just fine. She bit her lip and mulled over the matter while she worked to fasten bandages on Gabe and the mystery guy.

At some point, Harvey came over and started helping her out. It made the work go a lot quicker, and it was nice to have a helping hand.

When they were done, he placed a hand gently on her shoulder and looked at her. The light of the fire reflected in his eyes, giving them a warm glow. "You did great out there today," he said.

Sariah made a "humph" sound and turned her head away. "Yeah, so great I practically killed everyone."

Harvey put his hand on her chin and turned her head back around. "Hey! You're being a little hard on yourself, don't you think?"

Sariah sighed. "I couldn't even get a fireball straight.

You managed one just fine. Why can't I? Why do I always screw things up?"

"You don't always screw things up, you know." He shook his head. "You're too hard on yourself."

She gave him a weak smile. Sitting there with the fire in the background and the daylight starting to wane, he looked pretty comfortable.

Sariah leaned over and let herself lay against his shoulder. Harvey took his other hand and gently caressed her hair. It felt nice, and the weight of the battle started to fade away.

"Harvey?" she said, looking up at him.

He looked down at her and smiled. "Yes?"

Sariah bit her lip and hesitated. She was always saying the wrong thing to him, so she wanted to go slow. "You...you're..."

The sound of someone coughing interrupted her. Both of them looked up from their position to see who it was. It was the mystery man. He was waving his arms about and trying to sit up.

Sariah looked at the mystery man, then back at Harvey. Harvey was staring at the new guy. She frowned. The moment was lost. There was no point in trying to bring it back again.

The mystery man coughed again, then sat up. He blinked and rubbed his eyes a few times, then looked around in a daze.

"Easy now," Sariah said. She got up and walked over to where he was sitting. "You suffered a pretty heavy attack back there. You're lucky we showed up when we did."

The mystery man nodded once. "That I am," he said in a

gravelly voice. He coughed once more. "Thank you, young lady."

Sariah took a good, hard look at him then. He was tall. Taller than even Harvey or Gabe, but also lean, not broad and muscular like those two. He had graying hair at his temples and a full beard, but his face didn't look that old. Maybe mid-thirties at best. His eyes had the faintest tinge of green to them, a deep, forest green like that of new leaves.

"I'm Sariah." She stuck out her hand, then craned her neck toward Harvey. "That over there is Harvey."

Harvey waved one of his hands at the man.

Bear let out two sharp barks.

Sariah smiled and pointed at the dog. "And that is Bear. Bear did a lot of work saving you, too."

The man blinked another couple of times and stared at Sariah's hand for a moment before doing anything. Eventually, he took it and shook it vigorously. His hand felt soft and new, not calloused like she expected. Almost as if the man had never seen a hard days' work in his life. Which was odd for a person of his age, especially one out in the middle of nowhere.

"Thank you," the mystery man said slowly. "Especially you, Bear." He winked at the animal and gave him a big smile. Bear seemed to preen under the attention.

"The name's Vincent," he continued, returning his attention to Sariah. "I was just passing through here when I heard that magnificent creature over there and had to come check it out for myself."

Sariah looked in the direction Vincent indicated. He

was pointing toward the massive wolf that had almost ended all of them.

She furrowed her brow. "That monstrosity? The wolf was many things, but I wouldn't put magnificent on that list."

Vincent shook his head slightly. "I wouldn't expect city folk like yourselves to understand."

Sariah let out a slight chuckle. "Well, you're right on that one. I definitely don't understand."

"It's different out here, alone in the Alpenwood," Vincent continued. "I don't have many men for companions, so I've taken a liking to the animals instead."

Sariah nodded. "I guess I get that. Still, that wolf was bad news."

Vincent hung his head. "Indeed, it was."

Her eyes grew wide. "But I thought you just said-"

The older man raised a hand to her lips to tell her to be quiet. "Sometimes, we can both be right, you know."

She hung her head low. "I guess I get what you mean," she admitted after a moment. "He was a magnificent creature, but still a terrible one at the same time."

Vincent nodded. "Indeed, young lady, he was. He was quite the splendid wolf at some point. Alas, he'd gone rabid by the time I found him. I was hoping to tame him, but it wasn't to be."

The older man stretched his arms and tried to stand, but fell back down just as quickly. Sariah and Harvey both lunged forward to help him keep his balance.

"Easy now," Harvey said. "You lost a lot of blood in the attack. Might want to take it slow for a bit."

Vincent looked down at his torn clothing and the bandages wrapped around his chest like it was the first time he'd ever seen them. It probably was. He seemed a little flighty.

"I'm sorry, Mr. Harvey. I guess you're right."

Sariah turned and started rummaging in one of their packs. "Here, Vincent, let's at least get you some food. You must be famished." She held out a handful of rations.

He took them in one hand and covered her hand with the other. "Thank you, young lady. Your actions and kindness today will not soon be forgotten."

Sariah blushed. "Yeah, well, I was just doing what anyone in my position would have done for another."

Vincent looked at her oddly. "I'm not so sure about that, young lady. I've met many humans in my travels. Most of them are not as kind as yourself."

Her blush deepened even further. "Gee. Uh, thanks?"

The older man bowed his head. "You're welcome."

Sariah took out a couple more rations and the three of them ate in silence for a few minutes.

Eventually Harvey broke the quiet. "You said earlier that you were trying to tame the giant wolf over there?"

Vincent nodded.

"How did you plan on doing that?"

The older man's eyes rolled back into his head like he was trying to remember. "That's right. You wouldn't know my customs, would you?"

Both Sariah and Harvey shook their heads.

"That reminds me," Vincent went on. "Did either of you see a fox with a bright red tail running around in the area earlier?"

Sariah looked at Harvey and then back at Vincent. "A

fox with a bright red tail? Can't say that I have, sorry. But what does that have to do with anything?"

Vincent waved a hand at her dismissively. "Never mind. It's of little importance. I'm sure he'll return eventually. He always does."

Sariah cocked her head to the side. She looked at Vincent more intently, examining the claw marks on his head. "Did you hit your head harder than I thought? You're not making any sense."

Vincent backed his head away, then he let out a deep laugh. "No, young lady. I assure you my head is just fine. It's just been so long since I've spoken with a human that doesn't share my point of view."

She frowned at him. "You're still not making sense."

"I'm not, am I?" She shook her head. "No matter. I'm sure it will all make sense someday."

Sariah groaned. Why is it always the "someday" speech with older folks?

"Anyway, back to the wolf attack. It's a custom of my people to take animal familiars as friends for life. We treat them much like family members. When I heard there was a massive wolf out in these woods running amok, I feared the worst. I had to come check on it myself and see if I could calm the beast down and set it on a better path."

Sariah nodded, even though it still didn't make a lot of sense to her. "So you wanted to help the big bad wolf out?"

Vincent nodded. "Exactly. I wanted to see if I could fix whatever was wrong in his life that made him lash out the way he did. Alas, the wolf's mind was too far gone for me to do anything with it." He hung his head low as he said the last part.

Sariah put a comforting hand on his shoulder. "I think I get it. I mean, only so much, because that wolf also wanted to eat me." She gave him a stupid grin. In the background, she could hear Harvey chuckle.

The older man raised his head and gave her a weak smile. "You must think me crazy for even trying."

Sariah thought about that for a moment and shook her head. "No, I don't. You saw a wrong in the world, and you tried everything you could to correct it. What's so unusual about that?"

Vincent nodded at her once again. "You are quite wise for one of such an age, young lady."

"Please, it's just Sariah." She was starting to grow weary of all this "young lady" nonsense. It made her feel uncomfortable.

"Sariah, then." He smiled at her again, a little brighter this time. "That's a lovely name, by the way."

Her cheeks felt flushed. "Thanks, I guess."

Vincent looked at both of them and once at Bear, then he spread his gaze wide. "Well, it's about time that I should be going," he said suddenly.

Sariah got up and pushed him down. "Remember what happened last time you tried to stand? At least rest for the night. You can leave in the morning."

Vincent chuckled again. "That's right. Standing didn't go too well last time, did it?" Sariah and Harvey both shook their heads.

"Well, I'll just have to heal these wounds of mine first."

Harvey gave Sariah a dopey look. "He really did hit his head pretty hard in the wolf attack, didn't he?" he whispered.

But Sariah was staring at Vincent. He had removed his bandages and placed his hands on the worst wound. His eyes had gone full green and the man appeared to be in a trance-like state.

A moment later, his body started to glow in the dim light ever so slightly. It was faint and hard to catch, but there was definitely a glow.

She watched in amazement as Vincent's skin started to stitch itself back together, like time itself was reversing.

Harvey had seen this happen before when Gabe had healed him, so he wasn't overly surprised. Perhaps that there was another person with healing power, but watching it unfold was nothing new to him.

Sariah, on the other hand, had never actually watched the healing magics at work. She'd always looked away when Gabe had done it to her, but watching the healing unfold in front of her like this was mesmerizing. The soft motions even soothed her nerves.

Almost as soon as the healing magic had started, it stopped. Vincent rubbed his hands on smooth, fresh skin that stood where wounds had been.

Sariah's jaw practically dropped to the floor. She'd never known magic could be so wonderful to watch.

Vincent held out his hand. She took it and helped him to stand. He got up effortlessly, as though the wolf attack hadn't even happened.

Sariah's jaw was still partially open. "How did you?"

"Heal myself?" Vincent finished for her. She nodded once. "I've picked up a few tricks of my own in my travels." He pointed to where his wounds had been. "That was nothing. You should see me on a good day."

Harvey chuckled behind her. "Now that's something I'd like to see."

Vincent walked over to Gabriel. "Here, let me heal your friend as well. It's the least I can do."

Her heart leaped in her chest. "You'd do that?"

Vincent nodded. "You were quick enough to offer help when I needed it. Please let me return the favor."

He got to work, deftly moving his fingers over Gabe's scarred body. It glowed as the magic went to work once more. Soon enough, the magic stopped flowing and Vincent looked at both of them.

"He may be weak and need extra food for a day or two, but I expect he'll make a full recovery now."

"Thank you," Sariah said, blinking and smiling broadly. "I was worried about him. He doesn't normally sleep this long."

Vincent grinned. "Yes, well I'm sure he'll wake up soon enough. He'll probably be starving when he does. Healing can make people hungry."

Harvey snickered. "That sounds like Gabe, all right."

Vincent looked at Sariah. "You suffered some wounds as well. Would you like me to see to them, too?"

Sariah shook her head. "Oh no. There's no need for that," she insisted. "I'll heal just fine on my own. It's Gabe over there that I was most worried about."

Vincent tilted his head to the side. "Are you sure? It'll only take a moment."

"Well, if you're sure it's no trouble. I don't want to over-tax you."

The older man shrugged. "No trouble at all, miss, especially for someone as nice as you." He gave her a slight wink and she blushed a little, then he walked over to her and placed his hands over her injured leg.

"Do you mind if I watch?" she asked.

He gave her a quizzical look.

"You know, so I can learn how it's done," she added with a grin.

"Of course!" he replied. "By all means, do. Though it's trickier than it looks, I'll have you know."

With that, he got to work. She watched as his eyes turned a deeper shade of green and a small light jutted out from his outstretched hand. The light enveloped her injuries, eventually overtaking them completely as her leg was filled with a dizzying warmth that was all at once relaxing and intoxicating. As quickly as it had started, the deed was done and Vincent withdrew his hand.

Though she had tried to watch his movements, it all went too fast and she felt like she hadn't learned a thing.

"All good," Vincent told her. "Your leg should be in tip-top shape now." He got up and Sariah could have sworn she saw him hesitate trying to stand up fully, but then it was gone.

"Thank you," Sariah offered. She stared at her leg, which looked good as new, then back up at him. "I feel like I owe you now."

"Nonsense!" Vincent protested. He turned away and faced the trees. "Well, I suppose I really should be getting going. I need to find where Ferdinand has run off to."

"Ferdinand?" Harvey asked.

"Remember the fox I talked about earlier?"

Harvey gave him a knowing smile. "Oh yeah. Ferdinand, huh?" He furrowed his brow. "Maybe he doesn't like his name?"

Vincent scoffed at him, but Sariah chuckled a little. It was funny to think about an animal running away because it didn't like its name, even if the prospect was obviously causing their new acquaintance no small amount of stress.

The older man cleared his throat. "At any rate, I'll take my leave now. Should the two of you ever need help in the future, feel free to seek me out in the Eagle Woods to the east of here."

Vincent smiled at them both once, then his eyes flashed green once again and he turned and left, humming a strange tune all the while.

Sariah and Harvey stared at each other for a full minute before doing anything, wondering if they had really just witnessed all of that.

After a few minutes she shook her head to clear it. She might never really know for sure.

CHAPTER TEN

Padron inhaled deeply, taking in every whiff and scent he could of the brisk mountain air.

It was cold up in the mountains, even at this time of year, but he liked it. He missed it, even. Until now he hadn't realized just how much.

He caught the scent of a nearby pine tree and a smile crept upon his face. It felt good to be back in the mountains near home. Or at least, what he used to call home.

He wondered if it would still feel like home for probably the hundredth time since he'd started this journey.

Chatwick had been pretty good to him, at least up until recently. The company of the humans down there and the familiarity of mining were both nice, but they didn't hold a candle to The Heights.

He took a good look at his surroundings. The trees were starting to thin out, giving way to rocks and more rocks. Some would find that odd or unsettling, but it was just how this rearick liked it.

It had been weeks since he'd left Chatwick behind. For

a while, traversing through the forests in the lowlands, he'd thought maybe he'd never find his way back. The thought had proved wrong soon enough once he'd found his first mountain path.

The path he now walked was quite well-trod, in fact. Just a few more hours of travel and he'd be there. Craigston, the original home of all rearick - where all of them had come from at one time or another.

Most of them were still there, too. Sure, some had up and left for greener pastures after the Arcadian conflict, like he and his small crew had, but the majority of the rearick still lived here, holed up in their quaint mountain home.

He shook his head to clear it of the memories. He wasn't here to return. He was here to obtain information vital to Sariah and Harvey.

Those two kids were his life, now. He'd known them since they were precious little kids running around at their parents' feet. Hell, he'd practically raised Harvey ever since his mother had died. The poor kid had trouble staying at home since that incident.

And little Sariah? She had always been a little too rough and tumble for her parents to handle. She'd kept the company of the rearick every chance she'd got.

He steeled himself emotionally. Homecomings were good and all, but he had to keep those two at the forefront of his mind. They were his reason for coming all the way back out here. He had a mission to complete.

The rearick rummaged around in his pocket and his hand closed on the gemstones jingling around in there.

They were making an awful racket, swishing about to and fro. It was enough to drive a person mad.

Those gemstones were the main reason he was here. He needed answers about them. Who better to give those answers than the original miners of those self-same rocks? That is, assuming he was right about them. If he was, he shuddered to think about what it could mean for his quiet little town of Chatwick. The place would never be safe again if he was right.

Padron took out the gemstones and looked at them. In the daylight, the little whitish rocks glinted something fierce. They were almost pretty to look at, in a way. Almost, but not quite.

He returned them to his pocket a moment later and they resumed their jingling nonsense. He swore those stupid little stones had it out for him. Not that they were sentient, but they'd still managed to annoy him for at least half the trip out here.

At least the journey thus far had been rather uneventful. He hadn't even run into any people for the most part, but then he was traveling through largely uninhabited portions of forests and hilly land, so that wasn't really a shock.

He rounded another bend in the rocks and caught sight of smoke rising in the air not too far ahead.

The sight brought another smile to his lips. That little column of smoke looked like it was coming from a chimney. That meant civilization was not too far away.

Did the smoke and the house it came from belong to Craigston? He supposed he'd find out soon enough. No use thinking about it until it mattered.

As he walked, he wondered what changes might have happened in his absence. It had been at least five years since his last visit. That was plenty of time for things to change up if only just a little. Even for rearicks.

Another plume of smoke appeared on the horizon, and then several more.

Padron's smile became bigger. That looked like Craigston, all right. He was almost home.

He started practically running up the rest of the way, eager to step foot in his old hometown. He thought back to his own formative years in that very place as he picked up his pace. Running around outside the mine when he was just a wee lad or the first time his Pa had taken him to Ophelia's. That was a rite of passage right there.

Padron wondered if Ophelia's was still around. It had to be. Surely things couldn't have changed that much.

His belly growled at him as he thought about Ophelia's. It had been ages since he'd had a chance to sample her brew. Every rearick knew Ophelia had the best brew on Irth. It even rivaled some of the mystics' concoctions. Better, in a way, since it put hair on your chest. The mystics' brew couldn't say that.

A few feet further in, he started to see people mulling about. Even from this distance he could tell they were all rearick. Too short to be humans, and too much facial hair. Most humans weren't fond of long, flowing beards.

He'd never understood the custom of shaving oneself. What was the point of leaving your face exposed like that?

He could make out even more houses and people. Up ahead to the left was his first destination - Ophelia's.

His eyes lit up like a child on his birthday and he headed straight for the tavern's big doors.

Once inside, he took a moment to let his eyes adjust to the lower light. He took in a deep breath through his nostrils and the overwhelming scent of brew assailed him. A smile crept onto his lips. It was glorious.

Padron strode up to the bar and sat down on the nearest stool. He waited for the bartender to turn around.

When she did, a wave of recognition passed over her face. Her eyes became brighter and she gave him a warm smile. "Well if it isn't Padron, back from tha dead."

"Good to see ya, too, Ophelia."

"What brings ye back 'round these 'ere parts?" she asked him.

Padron's grin got wider until it stretched from ear to ear. "What can I say, they just don't have good brew in the lowlands. I had ta come back to tha source."

Ophelia shook her head. "Ye always were a bit of a joker, Padron."

He nodded. "Aye, but I did miss ye." His stomach growled again, loud enough for half the bar to hear it. "And I wasn't lyin' about missin' yer brew, woman. Get me a flagon before I start to disappear, will ya?"

"Aye, of course." Ophelia turned and poured out two massive flagons of ale, then turned back and handed them to Padron.

Padron took a big, long sniff of the stuff. It smelled like heaven, or at least what he imagined heaven must smell like if it was full of ale.

He took a big, long draught of the first pint, finishing almost half of it in the first gulp, then set the mug down.

There were frothy bubbles flecked throughout his beard. He cleared them off with one swipe of his hand and then let out a giant belch. He patted his belly which felt fuller and warmer in the same step.

Ophelia beamed at him appreciatively.

Yes, it was good to be home, all right. There were good folk here that he missed.

He looked around, then leaned forward. "The bar seems light today, darlin'. Where are all my miner folk?"

Ophelia shrugged. "They're around. Most a them are still diggin' at this hour. Yer early if you were hopin' to catch the crowds. Just wait around a bit an they'll all come a runnin' before long."

Padron nodded. It was still fairly bright out. He supposed maybe he had been a little early arriving into town. Which meant more time to enjoy Ophelia's ale, and that wasn't an altogether bad thing.

He took another drink of his mug. The brew felt good going down his throat. It tasted slightly of honey with a bitter after-kick, just like he'd always remembered.

Ophelia was busy doing something behind the counter, so he tapped on her shoulder to get her attention.

She seemed startled when she turned. "Yes, lad?"

"What's on the menu fer today? I could use somethin' a bit more substantial for the old tum while I wait for the miners ta finish their shifts," he said.

The bartender whistled to the kitchen in the back. "Hank! Get me a bowl of me finest stew!"

Hank shouted something unintelligible back at her.

A few moments later, a bowl of steaming hot stew was

delivered through a hole in the wall. Ophelia set it in front of him, then went off to tend to something else.

Padron looked at the bowl in front of him. The stew was mostly brown with some orange and green bits sticking out of it. He couldn't quite tell what it was made of, but the smell was mouthwatering, so he supposed it didn't much matter.

He took a spoonful of the stuff and shoveled it Harvey into his mouth. The meat was so tender it practically melted on his tongue. Hastily, he gobbled up the rest of the stew in as few bites as possible and gave another appreciative belch. Oh, how he'd missed Ophelia's cooking.

Afterward, Padron sat at the bar, nursing his remaining flagon of ale. He didn't want to drink it too fast, figuring he could have more later when the miners came in.

He didn't have to wait long. About an hour later, dirt-covered miners started pouring into the bar in droves, all ordering flagons of their own.

Padron scanned the incoming crowd for familiar faces but didn't see anyone he recognized. He frowned. Apparently, things really had changed, even if it didn't look like it on the surface.

He whistled for Ophelia again. "Hey, is Mortimer or Garrett still around?"

Ophelia shook her head and her eyes looked sad. "I'm afraid not. They both left a while back. No one's seen or heard from them in a while. Longer than ye've been gone from 'ere."

Padron frowned. He remembered the two fondly. Surely, they would have had the answers he sought.

"What about Walt? Is he still runnin' the mining operation?"

Ophelia chuckled. "Aye. That old coot ain't gonna leave the operation in charge of some runt. They're gonna have ta pry his corpse out a his seat when he passes on."

Padron joined in the laughter. That sounded like old Walt, all right.

"Any idea where I can find him at this hour?"

Ophelia nodded. "Right up the hill past the first mine entrance where he always is. I swear he never leaves his office these days. Probably fer the best. He's not exactly popular anymore." She made a vague waving motion with her hand in the direction he should travel.

"Aye, that sounds about right." He'd almost forgotten about the cave-in incident several years back around the same time as the Arcadian conflict. Many rearick blamed it on Walt's harsh rules at the time. He'd softened a bit since, but rearick opinions were slow to change.

Padron thanked her for the information, paid his tab and got up to leave. Ophelia mumbled something back, and he was on his way.

He stepped out of the bar and noted the sky was starting to get dark and the air was turning colder. He rubbed his arms to get some warmth into them. It had been quite pleasant back in the bar.

For a moment, he considered going back inside. Surely a night or two's respite wouldn't ruin anything. He shook his head and decided against it. He had a mission to complete. Everything else was just a momentary diversion.

He headed up the mountain trail in the direction Ophelia had pointed, not that he'd needed the directions.

His feet seemed to remember the route to the mines and Walt's offices just fine on their own. He'd walked those paths for years before he'd left Craigston.

It didn't take long before he had passed the giant opening to the first mine and was at the big double-doors to Walt's offices. They looked a little aged and scuffed around the edges, almost like the place had run down a bit while he was gone, which was odd. The mining operation up here had been quite lucrative still when he'd left.

He wondered why the place looked so old.

It didn't matter. This wasn't his home anymore. Even if he wanted to, he no longer belonged. He knew that in his heart.

Padron walked up to the doors and knocked on them hard and loud to make sure he was heard.

A moment later, he heard the sounds of footsteps on the other side shuffling about. Before long, the door swung open and a young female head popped out of the opening.

"Yes?" the young lady said.

Padron smiled at her. Her long, blonde hair framed her face, making her look quite attractive. Maybe it was the ale talking, but he quite liked what he saw.

"I'm looking for Walt. Heard I might find him up 'ere."

The young lady nodded. "Aye. May I ask what business ye have with him at this late hour?"

Padron was taken aback. He wasn't quite sure what to say. He hadn't expected the third degree from such a pretty face. Everyone in Craigston was usually so nice.

He thought about it for a moment. Should I admit my reason fer coming to this lass, or give a fake excuse?

Fortunately, he didn't have to ponder it long. Before he

could do or say anything further, a voice from further in the building called out to them.

"Is that Padron I hear out there?" the voice called.

Padron smiled. It was Walt's voice. "Aye, ye old coot! Now let me in 'ere already. It's bloody cold out!" he fired back.

There was the sound of feet shuffling again, then the young lady head ducked back into the room. There was the sound of muffled talking for a few minutes, and finally Walt's head protruded from the door frame instead. The older man had a broad grin on his face.

"Well bless my arse. It's Padron come back at last! We wondered if ye was dead or not."

"Ye can't fell me quite that easily. Make me soft 'round the edges perhaps, but that's all."

Walt held open his arms. "Come 'ere, you!"

Padron embraced the older man for a moment, then he was led inside.

"So tell me," Walt started. "What brings ye all the way back out 'ere at this time o' the year? Lookin' fer work?"

Padron shook his head. "Nothin' quite like that, no. I'm lookin' fer answers."

Walt let out a hearty laugh. "We ain't got hardly any o' them 'round these parts, sonny. Barely have work these days, even."

Padron frowned. "What happened?"

Walt sighed and motioned for the younger rearick to take a seat. "The Arcadian conflict's what happened. After that ended, most o' tha requests fer amphoralds dried up faster than yer mama's tit. We still get requests from time to time, but it's not like it used to be where we couldn't dig them out fast enough to keep up."

Padron hung his head. "I'm sorry ta hear that, lad."

Walt scoffed and side-eyed him. "Who're ya callin' a lad? I'm at least ten years yer senior!"

The two burst out laughing.

"Aye, ye are that, indeed," Padron answered once the laughter died down. "Actually, about them amphoralds. That's kinda why I'm back 'ere."

Walt's ears perked up. "Oh? Did ye find a new market fer them out there in tha lowlands somewhere?"

Padron shook his head. "Nothing quite like that, no, I'm afraid."

Walt's expression soured. "Ah well. Shoulda known." He snapped his fingers once.

Padron rummaged around in his pocket. "Actually, I was hopin' ye could help me identify these 'ere stones. I think they may just be amphoralds, too."

It took a minute, but he finally found the jingling gemstones and pulled them out. They sparkled a bit in the light of the room.

Walt gave a low whistle. "Them's some mighty fine gems ye've got carryin' around with ye," he said. "Let me have a look."

Padron handed over the stones. Walt's rough hand accepted them readily.

The older rearick produced a small glass device from one of his own pockets and placed it up against one of his eyes. He used the strange device to take a closer look at one of the stones.

"Hmm," Walt said. "What do we have 'ere?" He turned

the gemstone around several times, examining it from several angles, mumbling something unintelligible every few seconds.

A moment later, he handed the lot of stones back to Padron. "Those're amphoralds, all right, sonny. Where'd ye find them?"

Padron's face got serious. "A little mining operation in the Alpenwood of all places."

Walt's eyes rolled and he rubbed his chin thoughtfully for a moment. "The Alpenwood, ye say?"

Padron nodded.

"I didn't know there were even any good mines out there."

Padron grinned from ear to ear. "There weren't, until me crew moved in."

Walt burst out laughing again. "Ye always were a funny one, Padron. I've sure missed ye."

Padron nodded again. "Aye, I've missed ye, too. I should really get going. I've got ta get back before too long."

Walt shook his head. "Nonsense! Ye'll stay tha night at my place and that's final. I won't have an old friend be travelin' around in the darkness!"

Padron lowered his head. "Nah, I couldn't accept that."

"Of course ye could! I won't hear different!" Walt insisted.

He let out a long sigh. "All right, fine. But only fer one night."

Walt grinned from ear to ear. "Wouldn't have it any other way."

The next morning, Padron awoke late. He had a massive headache. Remembering the night before with Walt, he figured it was probably from the excessive amount of brew the two had imbibed.

He shook himself and rubbed his eyes. Daylight was creaking in through the window and it stung his eyes. He'd forgotten what the morning after a drinking binge felt like. The brew down in Chatwick wasn't hearty like the stuff up here. It didn't have the same kick. He could barely get a buzz off the lowland stuff.

Padron took a few moments standing, but once he was on his feet, he gathered up his belongings and went to check on Walt. The sop was still snoring loudly in his bedroom.

Padron left without any further words. He'd already overstayed his welcome. It was time to get back to his new family. He had information to impart. Information that could change everything.

He thought about the implications of this new information for another moment. Did Jeffrey, the mine foreman, know what they'd stumbled upon, way down in those mines? He had to, otherwise why would he have barred the area off. What would that mean for the rest of the town's inhabitants there was no way to know for sure.

Padron sighed once and kept moving. There was plenty of time to worry about all of that on the trip down, he supposed.

It wasn't until he was about halfway down the road from Craigston that he finally noticed his pack was a bit lighter. The amphoralds were gone, as was about half of his coin.

He shook his head. Craigston had changed. Or at least Walt had. He wasn't sure which. He thought for a moment about going back and demanding the old coot give him the gems back but thought better of it. Craigston was the past. It was high time he left it there.

CHAPTER ELEVEN

"Come on, slowpokes! We're almost there!" Sariah shouted back at her companions.

Mutters and a low bark from Bear were all she got in return.

She slowed down to match pace with Gabe for a moment and nudged him in the shoulder. "Pick up the pace already!"

Gabe let out a sigh and shook his head. "I'm still recovering, remember?" He pulled on his face. "That druid fixed me up nice and good, but I'm not at full strength yet."

"But we're almost there!" she whined. "If we go at our previous pace, we can reach Chatwick by tonight!" She pulled on his tunic. "Come on. It can't be that bad, can it?"

He let out another sigh. "All right Sariah, I'll try." He gave her a wry smile. "I just can't say no to you, can I?"

"That's what I like most about you," she said with a wink.

She started walking faster again and looked back to make sure Gabe, Harvey and Bear were keeping up this time. They all picked up the pace, though there was some more grumbling.

Her eyes scanned the horizon. Up ahead, through the tops of the trees, she swore she could see a hint of smoke from the town bakery. She thought about all the good food they made and it made her stomach growl. Suddenly, she wanted nothing more than to be home.

As she kept going, she happened upon a small clearing in the trees that hadn't been there the last time they'd been on this road.

That's odd, she thought. She shrugged her shoulders and kept going anyway. The pull of Chatwick and home-coming was too strong.

Harvey signaled a halt from the rear. "Hold up!" he called.

Sariah looked at him. His brow was furrowed, and his eyes looked narrow.

"What's up?" she asked him, walking over in his direction.

He sniffed the air. "Something's not right," he said slowly.

"Oh, you're just being superstitious," she chided him, lightly punching him in the ribs. "We're almost home. We know this area like the back of our hands. There's nothing to worry about."

Harvey rubbed his chin. "I know. But still, the air's off." He gave her a grim look. "I don't like it."

She looked at Gabe. He was looking weird, too.

"Look, I'm sure it's nothing," she insisted.

"I don't know," Gabe chimed in. "Maybe we should listen to the kid."

Sariah looked at both of them wild-eyed. She crossed her arms over her chest. "I don't know what's gotten into both of you, but I'm going home. If you want to join me, you're welcome to."

With that, she turned her back to both of them and marched forward.

"Sariah, wait!" Harvey cried, but it was too late.

She took another step and heard something clink under her foot, then felt a sudden pain as metal bit into her leg.

"Damn!" she swore. In spite of her resolve, she fell to the ground. Both Gabe and Harvey rushed to her side.

"What is it? What's wrong?" Gabe asked. He placed a hand on her shoulder and kneeled down next to her. Harvey took up a similar position on her other side.

Bear went around to the front and nudged her with his nose.

"I'm not sure," Sariah started. "I seem to have stepped on something." She pointed down to her leg.

Gabe pushed some vegetation out of the way to get a good look. He gasped, so she looked as well. Wrapped around her leg was what looked like an old-fashioned animal trap. Several gnarly, half-rusted teeth had sunk into her skin.

Harvey maneuvered his hands underneath her leg and deftly managed to disarm the trap. She felt the pain lessen as the teeth retracted, but the damage still looked severe.

"That looks pretty bad," Gabe said, shaking his head.

"You think?" she spat back at him, but it was her own fault for getting in this mess.

If only I'd listened to Harvey.

"How bad is it?" she asked.

Gabe grimaced and moved his hands over the tears in her leg. He poked at a few spots and she winced as he did so.

Harvey hovered over her as well, looking and pointing at certain spots and making weird expressions with his face all the while.

Gabe stood up and looked down at her. His eyes were grim. "I'm sorry to tell you this, Sariah, but I think we're going to have to amputate."

She looked for any sign or hint of a joke in his demeanor but found none. She gulped down the knot of fear that was forming in her throat. "Amputate?" she repeated, barely able to say the words.

Gabe looked once at Harvey, then back at her. He nodded once.

Sariah's face darkened and she let her gaze drop to her wounded leg. Her leg couldn't be that bad. She looked back up at Gabe and he was grinning like an idiot.

"Got you!" Gabe said. Then he burst out laughing and Harvey did the same.

Sariah's cheeks flushed and her frame softened. "Hey!" she quipped. "That wasn't very nice of either of you. You really had me worried for a minute."

Gabe winced and held up his hands. "Sorry, I just couldn't resist."

"Ugh." She shoved him gently. "So how bad is it really?"

Gabe smoothed out his clothes and straightened up. "Well, it's not that bad, but those teeth were pretty rusted. It might get infected. At the very least, you probably shouldn't try to walk on it for the rest of the day."

She felt relieved. "Okay. I can live with that."

"I'll just heal it real fast," he continued.

Sariah nodded once, then her thoughts turned to how warm and comforting Vincent's healing magic had been, and she thought about sharing that same feeling with Gabe. Looking up at him and imagining his hands on her with that warm glow all over them made the whole thing start to feel intimate.

Her cheeks started to flush, and she averted her gaze. Was she ready to feel that way with Gabe? And with Harvey watching?

"Is there another option?" she asked.

Gabe rolled his eyes. "Didn't you hear me? It's going to get infected. It needs proper care or it's going to get worse. Then we really might have to amputate."

She groaned. "Aww, man. Well, can't we just put some medicine on it or something?"

He shook his head. "Do you remember packing any medicinal ointments when we left Stratton?"

Sariah hung her head low and she blushed a little. She knew he was right.

"Yeah, I don't, either."

A memory from her past came to her. Something about using herbs from the forest to treat injuries. She'd been in a particularly rough fight with a neighborhood kid and had gotten scraped up pretty bad. Her mom had gone out into the woods and come back with some plants that she'd mushed up into an ointment to help the wounds heal.

The scene brought a slight smile to her lips. The little kid she'd scuffled with was Harvey. They'd become friends shortly after that incident.

Sariah looked up at Gabe. "Well, what about making an

herbal salve? Aren't there herbs in the woods that can help with this sort of thing?"

Gabe was shaking his head again. He sighed at her. She still found it kind of cute and annoying at the same time, even now.

"Maybe," he admitted. "If I knew what any of those herbs were, that is. But I don't. I use magic for my healing, remember? Why would I need to know about all those plants?"

Sariah groaned again, but he had a point. "Fine," she said. "I guess you can do it."

"Good," Gabe said. "Now, don't move. This will all be over quickly." He knelt beside her and got to work.

At first, she couldn't look at him and watched the forest floor instead, but as Gabe's hands started to warm up her leg, she found herself entranced by his motions.

Her eyes looked at his, turning green and looking sternly at her injury. She tried to imagine what he was feeling but came up blank.

Then the healing power hit her. It felt like home and birthdays wrapped into one and made her feel safe in a way she hadn't in weeks. She wanted nothing more than to fall into Gabe's arms and stay there.

As quickly as the power had come, it left. Gabe took a half a step back and sat down on a nearby fallen branch. "It's done," he said.

Sariah looked down at her leg. There was fresh, pink skin peeking out from the holes in the fabric the trap had left. There was no trace of any injury. She felt the skin with her hands. It was soft and smooth to the touch, like a newborn. It was truly a work of wonder.

She tried to stand, then and found she could do so quite easily. She tried taking a few steps and shaking her leg. It stood up to all of her tests.

"It feels much better now," she told Gabe.

He smiled at her. "You're welcome."

Part of her wanted to kiss him. Instead, she punched him square on the arm.

"What was that for?" he whined, rubbing the spot where she'd struck him.

She put her hands on her hips. "Nothing," she lied. She turned away before he could see her blush.

Gabe rolled his eyes. "Yeah, well you'll thank me for it tomorrow."

She peeked over her shoulder to look at him. He looked exhausted. The healing, on top of recovering from the wolf attack the day before, had really done a number on him. She started to feel bad.

"Hey," she said slowly, turning and walking toward him. "I'm...I'm so-"

Gabe held up a hand to shush her. "Don't worry about it." His eyes darted around the clearing and he started to waver. "I think maybe I'll take a break."

Sariah rushed in and grabbed him before he could fall over. "That sounds like a good idea." She helped him sit down on the ground, then patted him on the shoulder.

"How about I get you some rations and you just rest for a bit?" She bit her lip. "Chatwick can wait for tomorrow."

"Are you sure?" Gabe asked her.

Sariah started rummaging around in her pack for some food. She paused and turned and nodded at him. "I'm sure." She handed him a ration and watched him chew on it for a second. "And thank you. Really. I mean it."

The gates of Chatwick stood before them not a hundred meters away. They were still in the trees, but only barely. There was a wide, open expanse in front of them before the town gates.

Sariah frowned. There hadn't been this wide a gap in the trees the last time she'd been home. Of course, that had been a few months ago. A lot could have happened since then. It didn't necessarily mean the Dusk Ravens had moved in.

She looked at Harvey. "See anything out of the ordinary?"

Harvey rubbed his chin thoughtfully. "Nope, can't say that I do. The town looks normal to me from here. The front gates don't even look like they've been reinforced or anything."

Sariah nodded. "I agree. It looks the same to me, too." She pointed to one of the guards. "That looks like Tim. Why, he's been guarding the gates badly for ages now. There's no way the Dusk Ravens would have let him keep his job."

Harvey smiled back at her. "Ain't that the truth," he replied. "That guy is a terrible guard. They would have replaced him right away. Would have replaced all of them, in fact."

"Maybe we beat the Dusk Ravens here?" she asked her two companions.

Gabe was looking rather sternly at both of them. "It's possible, I suppose. Or they might not have been headed here. Still, my sources have never been wrong before." He shook his head. "It doesn't make any sense."

"What doesn't make any sense?" Sariah inquired.

"Why don't we see any sign of them? No banners, no troops at the gate, nothing. They should be here, but the town looks completely ordinary. Why?"

Sariah shrugged. "Let's take it as a good sign. We finally beat the bad guys at something."

Gabe was shaking his head. "Yeah, I don't think so. It doesn't work like that."

"Yeah, okay Mr. Cynical, whatever you say." She turned and faced the town, then took a big step forward. "I'm going to go head over to the gate and talk to Tim and see what's going on. That guy couldn't keep a secret if his life depended on it."

Gabe shot out a hand and grabbed her by the shoulder to stop her from going any further. "I don't think so. It's not safe for you. What if it's a trap?"

"A trap?" Sariah shook her head. "Tim is so bad there's no way he could be part of a trap."

But Gabe's expression was stern. Even Bear was looking at her with an air of disapproval.

"I'd rather you stay here," Gabe insisted. "They're after you, remember? Let me go ahead instead. I'll ask around and see what's going on. No one in Chatwick knows me, save for Padron. If there's something going on down there, I'll figure it out."

She groaned, but he had a point. No one knew him, but

her on the other hand - if it was a trap, she'd set it off for sure.

"Okay. We'll do it your way."

Gabe walked up to the gates of Chatwick, trying to look as unassuming as possible. He left everyone else behind, including Bear.

As he neared the two guards at the gates, he gave them a stiff salute. The one Sariah had not referred to as Tim saluted him back. Tim did nothing. He kept walking.

"Good afternoon, gentlemen," he called to them when he was only a few feet away.

Tim took a step forward. "Afternoon, sir. What brings you to this area of the Alpenwood today?"

Gabe shrugged. "It's a nice day. Beautiful weather. Thought I'd stop by and see if there were any good wares to be had at the local market."

Tim stepped forward and stood in such a way as to stop Gabe's advance. He put out a hand in front of him. "May I have your name, please, sir?"

Gabe stopped walking and gave him a broad smile. "Sure thing. The name's Gabriel. I live a few days away from here over yonder." He pointed off to the west, in the direction of his cabin. There was no sense in lying about it. If everything was normal, they'd know if he was lying. If it wasn't, then it really wouldn't matter soon enough.

Tim frowned at him. "Over yonder, you say?" He pointed in the same direction Gabe had.

He nodded at the guard.

"Hmm. I don't remember hearing about anyone living by themselves over there. You been in the area for a long time?"

Gabe shrugged again. "A few years, maybe. Not a super long time. I took over for my old mentor, Jakob. You might have heard of him?"

Tim shook his head. "Sorry, sir, but that name's not really ringing a bell."

He gave the guard a sideways glance. "Really? I thought Jakob was well known in these parts."

Now it was Tim's turn to shrug. "I suppose it's possible. To be honest, I haven't been a guard here for very long, so I wouldn't really know for sure."

"Ah," Gabe replied. "Fair enough. So, can I go to the market now?" He took another half step.

Tim pushed him back firmly. "I'm sorry, sir. The market is closed today. Town holiday and all. You'll have to come back some other time."

Gabe snapped his finger. "Oh, shoot. I heard they make the best mince pies around here, too," he said casually.

"Yes, well like I said, another time perhaps." Tim smiled at him through clenched teeth.

Gabe nodded at Tim. "Yes, another time." He shrugged. "I suppose I'll be on my way. Hope to see you again the next time I'm here."

He held out his right hand for the guard to shake it. Tim took the offered hand and shook it vigorously with one of his own.

When Gabe let go, he took a quick look down at Tim's palm, being as quick as he could. Just a half glance and then back up at Tim's eyes. It was short enough that Tim would hopefully not even notice.

He smiled at the guard known as Tim and turned and walked away back to the cover of the trees. Sariah, Bear, and Harvey were waiting for him with expectant looks.

"So?" Sariah asked.

Gabe shook his head slowly. "I don't know who that is in front of the gates, but it's sure not Tim. He didn't act anything like I remembered from the last time, doesn't know the area, and has never heard of Jakob."

Sariah and Harvey's eyes both grew wide in surprise.

"Worse - on his palm there's a tiny Dusk Raven tattoo. I caught a glimpse of it before I left." He placed a hand on Sariah's shoulder. "I'm sorry, but it looks like your town's not safe, after all."

"We have to do something!" Sariah exclaimed. "It's just two guards, we can take them!"

She started moving but Harvey held her back. "Wait. We can't just rush in there like this."

Sariah turned and looked at him. "Why not?"

"Because it's not just two guards! There could be hundreds of them in there," Harvey reasoned.

Gabe nodded. "The kid is right. They wouldn't let me into town. I'm not sure what all they're hiding, but there must be quite a few troops in there for them to deny me entry."

Sariah looked crestfallen. Her gaze traveled between Harvey and Gabe several times. "Well, we have to do something. We can't just let our friends and family suffer!"

"Don't worry," Gabe said. "We won't let them suffer for long. I have a plan."

Sariah's eyes brightened. "You do?"

"Mm-hm. We just need to wait until nightfall. Then we can sneak in like we did at the bandit camp and sack their leader."

Sariah groaned. That meant invisibility spells. If it was just to sneak in and not to kill, it wouldn't be too bad. At length, she nodded. "I guess we'll do it your way. So, what's the plan?"

The Master walked through the hallways of his stronghold. Unlike most, he knew the tunnels very well. He'd memorized them long ago. Even helped dig a few of them himself, though not very many.

Most of the complex had existed long before he'd decided to make the place home. It was a maze of tunnels underneath the ruins of an old city. Some of his underlings had complained that an underground lair was too obvious a spot to set up shop, but he disagreed. For some reason, none of their enemies realized this tunnel network even existed. Building underground was rare in these parts.

He was headed to his magic experiment lab. Today was an experimentation day. No business to tend to or decisions to make. Just him and his research.

A smile crept onto his lips. This was his favorite kind of day. He so loved dabbling in new powers, and he was close to unlocking a new secret. He was sure of it. He felt like he was right on the cusp of a major breakthrough.

On the way, he passed Daniel, his trusted assistant. "Good morning, Daniel," he said.

The assistant bobbed his head but said nothing. Such was Daniel's way. He only spoke when he found it necessary to do so. It was a trait he particularly enjoyed about the man. That and his ability to find him willing participants for his studies.

"Are there any new guests in the study today?" the Master asked his assistant.

Daniel nodded his head. "Yes, sir. There's one guest in there today. He's been waiting for hours just to see you."

The Master's smile grew wider. "Excellent. I trust you showed him an appropriate level of courtesy?"

Daniel nodded again. "Yes, sir. Just like you asked."

"Fantastic. I can always count on you, Daniel. Pray that remains the case."

With that, he left his assistant to do whatever he normally did during his downtime and he kept heading toward his lab.

His lab was what he referred to as his "library" with others. It sounded so much more inviting than to call it a prison laboratory. Who would voluntarily want to go into one of those? A library on the other hand - there were plenty who wanted to go to a place full of books and learning.

As for where he got his subjects, it was easy enough to come across willing participants if you framed the job correctly. One thing widely known about the Master was his talent and skill with the magic arts were beyond compare. Everyone wanted to learn directly from him, but few were ever chosen to actually do so.

He had so little time to devote to training, and he only took the very best as his students. The rest of the people who volunteered and showed even the slightest hint of talent were taken in as his special guests at the library, where they waited for their certain doom.

Since no one who got sent to his "library" ever made it out alive, there was never anyone around to spoil the deception.

At last, he was at the doorway to his lab. He opened it slowly and clapped loudly once to turn on the magitech lights within. They were an extravagance, yes, but a necessary one. He needed the light in order to operate properly, and there was no real ventilation in his lab, so torches were out. A victim's screams would have somewhere to escape to if there were vents.

He looked at the person chained to the wall. He was a decently sized chap. Maybe 5 feet 10 inches and around 200 pounds. He'd obviously lived a decent life up to this point and was likely accustomed to some of the finer things.

The Master smiled at his victim. "Good morning, Charles."

The man on the wall looked at him with fear in his eyes. He knew that he'd been tricked by now, but not by how much. "I'm not Charles," he said in a shaky voice.

The Master dismissed him with a wave of his hand. "It doesn't matter. All my special guests are named Charles now. It makes it so much easier for me to keep track of them that way."

He reached out and grabbed Charles's cheeks and gave them a quick squeeze. "Mm, you look like quite the nice subject. Well-fed. I'm assuming you had two loving parents, yes?"

Charles whimpered and tried to say something, but the Master waved him off again. "It really doesn't matter. You'll find I'm not really one for chit-chat while I'm working."

The Master looked his victim up and down once more. He noticed a wet spot on the man's pants and his face soured.

What kind of victim soils himself before the torture even starts? he wondered. He shook his head and chuckled to himself. This new breed of volunteers wasn't the hardy stock he'd grown accustomed to. He'd have to find a way to get some better people in here next time, maybe cast a wider net.

"Now, Charles, are you ready to get started? I know I am." He rubbed his hands together greedily, then placed one of his hands on Charles's exposed midsection.

"I do believe this is going to hurt you a lot more than it's going to hurt me. Ready?"

The Master didn't wait for an answer. The magic started pouring out of his hand and into Charles's body. Unimaginable pain rocked poor Charles, and he screamed louder than he'd ever screamed in his entire life. It was a long time before the room was quiet again.

CHAPTER TWELVE

Gabe looked at his two students, then down at Bear. "Now remember Bear. You have to stay out here. You're too noisy for a stealth mission."

The dog let out a whine, then bowed his head and laid down in the grass.

"I know, Bear. It hurts me, too. You can come on the next mission, promise." That seemed to mollify the animal.

He looked at Sariah and Harvey again. "Do you remember the plan?"

They both nodded. "Yes, we remember," Sariah said. "Don't worry, we won't screw it up. Just make sure you do the same."

Gabe laughed a little. "Me, screw it up? It's my plan! Believe me, I've got this one in the bag."

Sariah smiled at him. "I believe you."

"All right, it's focus time. It's going to be a long night, and that's only if everything goes to plan."

She nodded once. "Yes, let's get a move on. Our friends have suffered long enough."

"Good. Now zip it. Remember, we need absolute silence for this to work."

Sariah and Harvey nodded at him again.

Gabe let out a sigh and took a deep breath. This was going to be a tricky evening. The Dusk Ravens had been fooled by invisibility once before. They were going to be on higher alert this time. He said a silent prayer to the Patriarch in hopes everything would work out okay.

He looked up at the sky. There was no moon, which was both good and bad. It would hide their movements even more, but it also gave them less light to work with. Since the plan relied on invisibility, there wouldn't be a chance to cast any light of his own.

He cast an invisibility spell over the three of them and they got moving. They approached the city gates slowly, trying to keep an eye out for anything unusual. For all they knew, there would be traps laid in the clearing for unsuspecting feet.

It's what he would have done if the tables were turned.

The trio made it about thirty meters before the guards at the gate started to come into focus. There were three guards now instead of the regular two and something else besides them. What it was, though, he couldn't quite tell.

He motioned for Sariah and Harvey to stop in their tracks while he moved closer. He made it perhaps another ten or fifteen meters before he saw them. Dogs. Big, gnarly-looking beasts that put poor Bear to shame.

These animals looked like sniffing hounds. Good at tracking scents.

"Scheisse!" Gabe swore under his breath. He headed

back to the other two and forced them all back into the forest.

Once they were there, he dropped the invisibility spell and looked at his companions. "This is bad, guys. They have dogs." He pulled on his face and swore again. "We need a new plan."

"What we need is a diversion," Harvey said. "Something to draw their attention away from the main gate so we can slip in unawares."

Gabe side-eyed him. "Well yeah, that much is obvious. Got any suggestions?"

Harvey rubbed his chin thoughtfully. "Not really, no. Nothing that's not suicidally stupid at least."

Gabe chuckled. "Well let's save that for the absolute last, okay?"

Sariah chimed in. "I may have an idea. There's a spot where the wall is weaker. Or at least, it used to be weaker. I used to play around in the area when I was younger. There's still a wall there, so it wouldn't be guarded or anything. We might be able to break through and make our way in."

"Yeah, but we'd still need to break through a wall. I don't know about you, but I left all my wall-destroying equipment at home," Gabe shot back.

Sariah shook her head. "It's really weak. You could probably burn through it with one really well-placed fireball. Only..."

"Yes?"

"Well, even that would cause a lot of noise. So, we'd still need a distraction."

"Which puts us back at square one."

"How long do you think it would take you to scout the area and break through the wall?" Harvey asked suddenly.

Sariah shrugged. "Ten minutes, maybe?"

Harvey smiled. "Then I have an idea. You two go to your area of the wall. When you hear a loud noise, do your thing."

Just like that, Harvey ran off into the woods.

"Wait!" Sariah called after him, but it was too late. He was gone.

Sariah and Gabe crept through the grass. They were headed toward the weakness in the wall she'd pointed out to him earlier. Gabe had recast his invisibility spell so they could move through the non-wooded areas with ease.

A knot of fear formed in Sariah's chest, but she forced it down. It wouldn't do her any good to get scared now.

She thought about Harvey and wondered what that fool boy was doing. He was going to end up getting himself killed if he wasn't careful. Bear had gone after him, so at least he wasn't completely alone, and Bear was a good attack dog. He'd keep Harvey safe.

A few moments later, they arrived at the weak spot in the wall. Sariah poked at the wood with one of her hands. It creaked and gave way fairly easily. She pointed it out to Gabriel, who nodded.

"You're right," he whispered. "That should fall pretty easily."

Sariah nodded. "What now?"

"Now we wait for that diversion."

———

Harvey ran through the woods away from the direction Sariah and Gabe had gone. He wanted to stay somewhat near the main gate, but far enough that if anyone came after him, he'd have a good head start.

A moment later, he heard the sound of barking from behind him. His blood froze.

Have they come for me already? he wondered. He didn't know how they'd even know where he was.

He turned to face the threat head-on.

Bear's happy mug greeted him. The dog let out another bark and then licked his hands with his tongue.

Harvey reached down to scratch the animal's head. "Good to have you with me, Bear," he said. "You know, sometimes I think you might just be the best out of all of us."

Bear yelped appreciatively at the scratching and the kind words.

"Don't tell Sariah that. She still thinks she's my favorite." He smiled down at the dog.

What am I doing? he thought. Here I am on a dangerous mission and I'm joking with a dog. Get your head on straight, kid.

He knew he was just stalling. The idea had sounded grand in his head. Cause a big disturbance far away from

Sariah and Gabe so all the guards would assume there was only one strike point and they'd all come running for him.

It would give Gabe and Sariah a nice head start to get in there and find the bandit leader.

All in all, it was a sound plan. There was only one problem. He didn't know what he was supposed to do once everyone came running for him. He wasn't that good at hiding, and he certainly couldn't cast invisibility yet. He'd tried, and like all mental magic, had failed spectacularly. That was the part that had him hung up right now.

It was too late for regrets. He just had to hope for the best.

He looked at the gate. There was a pretty big overhang of wood at the top. If he aimed a big enough fireball for the middle, he should be able to dislodge some of it. That would certainly get the guards running. It was a bold plan. He said a silent prayer to the Patriarch it would work.

Harvey patted Bear's head once for good measure and focused intently on his magic. His eyes turned coal-black to match the night as he worked.

A moment later, he had his fireball. He threw it forward with all his might. It hit the top of the gate dead-center with a loud boom and wood came raining down.

Not two seconds later, he heard another, smaller explosion.

That must be Sariah and Gabe, he thought. He could only hope that everyone would be too distracted by the bigger explosion to notice.

The guards looked stunned for a moment, then one of them came running in his general direction. He was followed closely by a column of well-armed guards soon after.

Harvey blinked a few times. His plan had worked! They were all headed straight for him.

He grinned like an idiot, feeling like a king among men for being successful. Then he did the only other thing he could think of - he ran.

Severin rocked back and forth in his chair. He was sitting on the second floor of a building near the middle of Chatwick.

His troops had arrived in town a few days ago and had taken over easily. The place had rudimentary guards who didn't even know how to do their job properly. It was obvious they'd never seen combat. Which worked well for him, since it meant he didn't lose any troops in the process of taking over.

From there, it had been a fairly simple process of building a small fortification to act as his base and replacing the gate guards with a few of his own.

He'd even allowed one of those magic types to come along with him. The guy was half-decent at mental magic and swore he could make his face look like anyone else. He'd had the guy play the part of one of the original town guards. That way, when the stupid little bitch came running back home, she'd think all was well and fall into his trap.

A cruel, wicked-looking smile crept across what was left of his lips, giving his face an even more ghastly appearance. This is so much better than straight recon, he thought. The Master will be pleased when I take her out, he thought.

Now all he had to do was wait for the doors of the trap to spring, and that should happen soon enough. He'd made plenty of a ruckus when he'd left the Stratton area to make sure someone picked up the news. Even a deaf beggar in a back alley should have heard it.

So here he was, sitting in his office awaiting news of Sariah's arrival.

He smiled as he thought over the thoroughness of his plan. He'd thought of everything down to the last detail. There was no way anyone was getting in or out of Chatwick without him knowing about it in advance.

Yes, the Master would be quite pleased with him upon his return. He'd definitely give him back the Stratton operation. Maybe even give him a promotion or let him expand his territory.

He heard the distinct sound of an explosion from outside the main gates and shot up, looking around confused.

Was that haughty little bitch really stupid enough to make a frontal assault? he wondered. It seemed unlikely. Still, he could take no chances. This was his shot to prove himself. He wasn't going to let it slip between his fingers.

"Marcus!" he called into the hallway behind him.

A lone guard peeked his head into the room. "Yes, sir?"

"Take a small contingent of guards and go investigate that explosion. Looks like we're under attack."

Marcus nodded and started to head out.

"Oh, and Marcus?"

The guard turned his head. "Sir?"

He made a knife motion over his neck. "Kill whoever was responsible."

Marcus got a wicked smile on his face. "Yes, sir."

Sariah and Gabe crept through the hole in the wall. They were still invisible as far as she knew, so she didn't bother being overly cautious about it and neither did Gabe.

She took a look around. The area was dark, and no one was mulling about. Undoubtedly, the town citizens were all in their beds, or maybe worse. No one seemed alarmed, and that was a good thing.

They both scanned the area for guards but didn't see any. She breathed a sigh of relief. Part one of her plan was complete. Now they just needed to find the bandit leader.

She started forward and on the way, she prayed for Harvey. He'd taken a big risk drawing the guards' attention like that. She hoped he'd come out of it safely. She didn't want to be the cause of losing anyone else she cared about.

Unconsciously, she looked at Gabe. He was taking quite the risk, too, coming with her like this. Would he live through the night, and if he did, what then? He'd certainly risked as much as Harvey. Maybe even more.

The two kept going and she shook her head. She'd think of a way to make it up to him later. For now, she needed to focus. They were getting closer to the town center now. Sariah figured that's where the Dusk Raven leader would have set up shop. It was a highly defensible position, and it would give him a good view of the whole town.

Up ahead, she spotted a lone guard. It was the first one they'd come across. He was walking up and down the alleyway just in front of them.

Sariah looked around. There wasn't anyone else close by. They could dispatch this guard, and none would be the wiser.

She paused for a moment, wondering if she could take him out being invisible, and if that made her as bad as them.

Still, it was him or them when it came down to it. Deep down she knew she'd have to cross this bridge at some point. She'd hoped to wait a bit longer, but there was no going back.

Now or never. She drew forth a dagger and stepped closer to the man.

Before she could strike, Gabe put his hand on her arm and held her back.

Was he having second thoughts, too?

The answer came soon enough. She noticed his hand was pointed off to the left.

Her eyes went to where his hand was pointing. There was another guard she hadn't seen.

She cursed herself for not being more thorough. If she'd moved on this guy without the other one being taken out, he surely would have raised an alarm.

Gabe made a motion with his hands as if to suggest splitting up and taking them both on at once. She nodded. He moved stealthily down the alley toward the guard on the left, while she closed in on her original target.

When she was only a few feet away, she stopped and waited for Gabe to get close enough to his own mark. Then, in one quick motion, they both struck, felling their guards at the same time.

Hers made a slight gurgling noise as she severed his vocal cords, but at least he didn't yell. She wiped the dagger off on the guy's uniform and put it back in its sheath. There was a slight queasiness in her stomach. She looked at Gabe. He gave her a thumbs up, which eased her nerves a little.

That's two down, she thought. Only like a hundred left to go.

Sariah and Gabe resumed their forward creep, going even slower. They were starting to come into a more populated area of town and had to be super careful so as not to raise any suspicion.

They crossed another few streets and then they were at the town center. In the middle of the town square, a brand-new building had been constructed. It looked about three stories tall, and it towered over the other buildings.

There was no doubting it. The Dusk Raven leader would be stationed within. There were only about a half a dozen guards in between them and its foreboding doorway.

Sariah looked at Gabe and smiled. There was a hint of anticipation in his eyes. She nodded once at him, and he nodded back. Together they advanced.

Severin tapped his foot impatiently. It had been a good twenty minutes since he'd sent Marcus and his troops out to investigate the explosion, and not a single one of them had come back yet.

What the hell is taking so long? he wondered. Just what in the nine hells is out there, anyway?

His expression soured even further. It wouldn't do him any good to sit around wondering. He'd have to do something about it.

He walked over to the wall of his new command complex and took his sword down from off the wall. He ran one of his fingers along the blade. It was nice and sharp. The blade had recently come back from the blacksmith, in fact, and he was eager to get the blade wet with fresh blood. He eyed the sword critically. Was that a crack in the middle? It was hard to tell, for the blade held an intricate design.

He gave the sword a couple practice swings and smiled. It was still perfectly weighted for combat. The blacksmith had done a good enough job, he supposed.

Severin looked out the main window in his complex down at the troops below. Everything seemed to be in order.

What was taking Marcus so long? He scowled again and headed for the doorway. It was time to take matters into his own hands.

That's when he heard the sounds of shouting and fighting coming from below.

Sariah watched as Gabe yelled and took on his closest attacker. He took the man's arm clean off with one broad stroke of his blade, cutting through the leather armor and bone like it wasn't even there.

Then he turned and took on another one of the guardsmen, knocking him to the ground with another couple of quick strokes. The guard fell, bleeding from a gaping wound in his chest.

It was a marvel to watch. The man moved like a machine between his assailants, cutting them down before they even had time to react.

At first, she thought it was because they were still invisible, but when she saw one of them parry his blows and mount a defense, she realized that was no longer the case.

Gabe was just that good.

A moment later, all six guards at the doorway were dead and broken on the ground. Gabe looked around with a wild look in his eyes, almost daring anyone else to take him on.

Sariah was stunned. She walked up to him and put one hand on his arm. "That was amazing."

Gabe let out a single bark of laughter, then his expression went serious again. "There's more of them coming. These ones look better prepared." He pointed with the tip of his blade to the next wave of attackers.

Sariah scanned the group. There were easily a dozen of them. Gabe was right, they looked much better armed and prepared than the previous group.

She stood next to Gabe and tightened the grip on her blade. "We can take them," she said.

He scoffed. "I've got this. You go after their leader." He nodded up the stairway.

Her stomach churned in anticipation and worry for Gabe. "Are you sure?"

Gabe shook his head. "No time to argue! Just do it!"

She worried for a moment about whether he could really take them all on, but he was right. This was their chance. She had to take it. She bounded up the stairs as fast as her feet could carry her. Behind her, Gabe let out another battle-cry as steel clashed on steel.

Harvey and Bear kept running. His little ruse hadn't bought him nearly as much time as he'd hoped, and all the guards were now chasing him.

He spared a quick glance over his shoulder.

"Scheisse!" he swore. The guards were catching up. One of them must have spotted him running through the clear part of the field.

He was in the woods now, but that was only a minor consolation. There were easily a hundred of them and only one of him. No matter which direction he headed, there was a good shot one of them would pick the same path.

Distance was his only hope, and his lead was draining away fast.

Harvey took another look behind him. There was a guard carrying a torch not twenty feet away and closing in fast. That torch would let him see far better than Harvey could in this darkness.

He kept going anyway. Maybe if he was lucky, the

guard with the torch would pick a different route far away from him.

He wasn't lucky. The guard kept heading straight his way.

Harvey said another prayer to the Patriarch and gulped down a knot of fear that had formed in his chest.

He decided to stand and fight. Out here in the woods, he had the upper hand. Maybe he could take a couple of them out before they got to him. Heck, maybe as many as a half a dozen. It was better than dying with an arrow sticking out of his back.

Harvey took out his sword. He looked down at Bear. The dog was looking up at him with big, teary eyes. It was like he knew it was the end of the line, too.

"It was sure nice knowing you, Bear," he said to the animal.

Bear inclined his head and licked his free hand.

"Yeah, I love you too, you mangy mutt." He gave Bear a weak smile.

He waited for the guards to come, and come they did. Not a moment later, the guard with the torch came crashing through the trees right in front of him.

Harvey stared him down. For a second, it was hard to tell which one of them was more scared of the other.

He let out a battle cry and lunged forward. The guard with the torch raised his blade in defense, but Harvey's blow never landed.

Something unseen came up to the guard from behind and swiped him off his feet. The guard fell to the ground, screaming and shielding his eyes from some unknown attacker. Harvey caught a glimpse of something red - blood maybe? - then the guard stopped moving.

Harvey did a double take. Had the forest just come out to help him? He shrugged. It didn't really matter.

A moment later, another couple of guards came crashing through the trees, weapons bared.

He'd been lucky once, but he wouldn't be so lucky again. This was it. He shouted at them, and tried to advance but suddenly couldn't move. He felt the distinct feeling of hands from above, then marveled as both he and Bear got pulled up into the top of the trees.

Sariah stopped briefly at the top of the stairs. The doorway was open and there was a man inside the room. He was turned so he could face the window and she couldn't tell who it was.

The man in the room let out a hearty laugh. The sound was gravelly and hoarse like it was painful to complete it.

"So, you've come at last," the man said. "Though not the way I thought you would."

The man turned to face her and Sariah's blood froze. It was the same bandit leader from the camp back in Stratton. The one with only one eye. If it was possible, he looked even worse than before.

A knot of fear formed in her stomach and she did her best to force it down, but it held on strong. The man had been menacing enough when she'd had the element of surprise. She no longer had that, now.

"Come in," Severin beckoned. "I won't attack until you do."

Sariah nodded once and inched her way into the room. She didn't trust him one bit. Bandits weren't known for their honesty.

Severin cracked his neck muscles and stared at her. His one eye seemed to bore through her head into her very soul. "Ready? Then come at me," he insisted.

Sariah tightened the grip on her blade. She could sense it was a trap. Severin must be very confident in his abilities if he was acting like this. Still, the longer she stood there, the more her nerves got to her.

Almost without thinking, she struck. It was a low blow, aimed at his foreleg. She didn't put a lot of force in the swing. It was more just to see him in action.

He parried the blow with ease. The power behind his parry went up her arm and shocked her hard enough she almost dropped her own weapon.

Severin smiled at her. "Good. Now let's finish this thing."

He came in with a broad swipe at her midsection. She leaped backward in time to dodge it, but not by much.

That was followed by another swipe at her sword arm. She brought her blade to bear in time and the two weapons clashed. Again, the force behind his blow was immense and she had trouble keeping a hold of her weapon.

She tried a vertical swipe aimed near his arm, hoping to get lucky. He batted it away like he wasn't even trying.

Her fear intensified. The man was good. Too good. Much better than her. She needed to get lucky or fight dirty.

Severin came in with another even thrust aimed at her outstretched arm. She managed to parry this, too, but not completely and she suffered a slight cut to her forearm.

Her flesh stung and she bit against the pain, but the movement gave her some time to act. She reached down to her belt with her free hand and pulled out a dagger. Lucien's dagger.

Then she made a broad sweep at Severin's midsection with her sword to open up a hole in his defenses and let the dagger fly. The sword stroke missed, but the dagger embedded itself deep into his gut.

Severin backed up a half step. He looked down at the dagger in disgust, then he pulled it out and tossed it onto the ground. He growled at Sariah, then advanced again.

He came in with another series of powerful blows. The wound in his gut seemed to be slowing him because she was having an easier time parrying and holding on at the same time. But only a little.

She saw an opening and went for it, making a wild lunge toward his head. The lunge went wide and hit nothing, but when she pulled her sword back, it smacked right along the side of Severin's blade and managed to snap the thing clean in half.

Severin looked at his broken blade and grunted. He moved faster than she would have thought possible and punched her in the gut.

This time, Sariah went to the ground, and her sword went flying.

He got on top of her and pressed down on her chest with one of his knees to pin her to the ground.

"I've got you now, you stupid bitch."

Sariah struggled against the bigger man's weight, but it was too much for her. He had her trapped. She was stuck.

He came at her then with a blow to her face. Her eyes blurred for a second and she swore she could see stars.

She felt something warm gush in her mouth, like a rush of blood from a loose tooth.

He hit her again, and her vision blurred even further. She wanted to pass out.

Severin grabbed her neck, then, and started to squeeze. She felt light-headed. She could feel the life leaving her body.

She needed to act fast. She was out of weapons, and Severin had the upper hand.

A thought came to her, then. It was a desperate ploy, but it was all she had left.

With all the force she could muster, she conjured a fireball and sent it careening into Severin's body.

This one was far larger than the ones on her previous attempts and had a lot more force behind it.

Severin flew off her and landed against the far wall next to the window. He looked down at his chest and saw it was on fire.

The big man stood and tried to put out the flames, but Sariah was ready. She got up on one knee and conjured another fireball, letting it fly into him.

Severin fell backward out the window and to the ground, burning and screaming the whole way down.

A few moments later, when her vision started to clear and her head stopped pounding, she got up and went over to the window. She looked down at the ground below her.

There, in the middle of the town square, was the

burning body of Severin - twisted, mangled, and very much dead.

Gabe looked up at her through the window. He smiled and gave her a salute, then pointed to a column of fleeing men.

Sariah looked at them. Those were the Dusk Ravens. They were running for their lives from some very pissed-off-looking townsfolk in robes and pajamas.

A smile crept upon her lips. Her town was safe once again.

CHAPTER THIRTEEN

Sariah looked at Gabe somewhat awestruck. While she'd been taking on Severin, he'd been fending off a horde of Dusk Ravens.

Miraculously, he didn't seem to have a single scratch anywhere on his body.

It was certainly possible he had healed himself, but his clothes didn't seem to have any new holes in them, either. Watching him fight had been a sight to behold.

She caught him looking at her and she turned her head and looked away shyly. His eyes were different tonight. There was a hunger or longing there that hadn't been there before. She supposed it could be from the earlier combat. She didn't really know what combat did to men.

Besides, she had other things on her mind, like Harvey. Chatwick was safe, and Gabe was fine and sitting by her, but no one had seen Harvey or Bear yet. They were still out in the woods somewhere, alone.

Were they dead? She shook her head. That was unlikely.

She would have known if that were the case, but they weren't back home with her, either.

She reached out with her magic to try and sense them but came up empty. That didn't mean much. She still wasn't the best at magic, after all, though she was steadily improving, and the recent bout with Severin had given her quite the confidence boost.

At the edge of her vision, she saw a man walking back toward town, carrying a few bags. For a split second, she thought maybe it was Harvey, but it was someone else.

It took a moment for them to come into focus in the darkness of the night, but soon enough she could make him out. The man was none other than Jackson, the town priest.

He approached the two of them. There was a stern expression on his face.

Sariah's eyes lit up. "Did you find him?" she asked.

Jackson shook his head. "We found these packs a short distance in the woods. They look like yours and Harvey's. But no, we found no sight of him or a dog. I'm sorry."

Sariah dipped her head.

Jackson put his hands on her shoulders and looked into her eyes. "Hey. We'll find him. He's a part of this town, too. We won't stop until we do."

Sariah nodded. "I'll go with you!" she offered.

Jackson held his hands out in front of him. "No, Sariah. You stay here."

"But!"

"But nothing!" Jackson frowned at her. "Look, we've got a dozen search parties out there. He will be found. Make no mistake. We won't leave him out there by himself." The priest's expression softened. "You go get some rest. You earned it. You took out their leader, you and your friend here. The two of you must be exhausted after a battle like that." He rummaged around in his pockets for a moment and produced a shiny object.

"Here, take the key to my house. Go in and make yourself comfortable. I'll let you know the moment the situation changes."

Sariah wanted to argue, but she came to realize he was right. She was tired, and likely wouldn't be a lot of help out there right now. Besides, she could trust Jackson to help her out in a time of need. He was their priest, after all. He wouldn't let her down.

At length, she nodded. "All right. I'll go to your home and wait."

Jackson smiled at her and ruffled her hair. "That's my girl." Then he turned and left.

Sariah looked up at Gabe. He still had that odd look to his eyes. It was strangely arousing. "Shall we?" she asked him, holding out her arm.

Gabe simply nodded and took her arm in his.

Harvey blinked his eyes. A moment ago, he'd been on the forest floor, about to fight for his life next to Bear. Now, the two of them were in the treetops silently watching throngs of Dusk Raven soldiers mill about looking for him.

On his left was the person who had saved him. It was none other than Vincent, the old guy they'd saved from the wolf attack two days ago.

The guy had a big, dopey grin on his face and a finger on his lips, begging Harvey to be silent.

He obliged. While he might be brash at times, he wasn't stupid. If he made any noise, he'd give away their position, and he was in no hurry to do that.

Still, his mind buzzed with questions. How had the old man lifted him into the tree? And how had that soldier died? Why weren't any of the soldiers more suspicious?

He would have to wait for answers until it was safe to talk.

He watched for what felt like an hour as the Dusk Raven soldiers skulked about. Hesitantly at first, and then later in droves like they were running from something.

Every now and then, a lone soldier would slip and fall and not get back up again. It was surreal to watch.

After what felt like hours, the coast was clear and there were no more Dusk Raven soldiers in the area.

He looked at Vincent. "Well first of all, thank you."

Vincent nodded. "It's what anyone would have done. Besides, I owed you a debt. Consider the favor repaid."

Harvey chuckled. "Fair enough. But how did you?"

"Lift you up here?" Vincent offered. "Hide us from the guards?"

Harvey nodded. "Yeah. That."

Vincent gave him a critical look. "How can you, with all your experience, really still have any doubts about it? It was magic, of course. Maybe not the kind you city folk are used to, but magic all the same."

Harvey thought about it for a moment. "I guess that makes sense. But when I use magic to lift things, they just lift. I could have sworn there were hands on me."

Vincent chuckled a little bit. "Is that what it felt like? Branches, more like. The trees lifted you up here to protect you."

Harvey looked confused. "The trees saved me? But why? How?"

Vincent shrugged. "Because I asked them to, silly. I saw you struggling down there and thought you could use some help. It seems the trees agreed with me."

Harvey was taken aback. "You talked...to the...trees?"

"In a way, yes." Vincent smiled again. "Though to be honest, they're not the most vocal bunch."

Harvey blinked and rubbed his eyes. "I had no idea magic could do all that."

"Oh son, magic can do many a wondrous thing that you've never dreamed of." Vincent grinned at him. "That was just the tip of the iceberg."

He pressed the subject. "What about all those soldiers who got attacked. Was that the trees, too?"

Vincent made a dismissive motion with his hands. "Nah, that was good old Ferdinand. He wasn't lost after all, just had a different idea of where to go."

Harvey's eyes grew wide. "Ferdinand did all that?" He scratched his chin. "I'll admit, I thought he was imaginary."

Vincent laughed a good, hearty laugh. "Better not let Ferdinand hear you talk that way, son. If it wasn't for his insistence, I wouldn't have even been in the area tonight."

Harvey smiled back at him. "Well tell Ferdinand thank you for me, then."

Vincent nodded. "Indeed I will. Next time he comes around. You should probably be getting back to your friends. I'm sure they're worried about you."

Harvey nodded. "Thanks again, and yes, I will!" He furrowed his brow. "Only...how do I get down from here?"

Sariah fumbled with the key and the keyhole in the dark. "Come on, you stupid thing, go in already. You know you want it."

Gabe stood by her, gently shaking his head. "I could make a light for you, you know?"

She shrugged. "I can handle a simple lock, thank you."

He backed up and threw up his hands.

She gave the key a turn. "There. That should do it." She pushed on the door and it opened, revealing a rather spacious living and dining area.

"Dang." Sariah let out a low whistle. "That priest sure does live the high life, eh? Maybe I picked the wrong profession."

Gabe walked in and looked around. "Looks nice, all right." He turned to Sariah. "We should probably get some sleep. It's late and I don't know about you, but I'm kinda tired."

Sariah's eyes drifted in his direction. Looking at him standing there in the living room, with the sheen of battle still on him, the last thing she wanted to do was go to bed.

Besides, she still needed to reward him somehow for his help.

She shook her head. "Nonsense. You must be famished. I'm sure Jackson has some food around here and I can't imagine he'd mind if we ate a bit of it. Let me cook dinner for you."

Gabe put a hand out in front of him. "Oh no, I couldn't trouble you."

She smiled back at him. "It's no trouble. Please, I insist."

He sighed. This time it was far more cute than annoying. "Well, okay, if you must. But at least let me help."

She batted her eyes at him. "Okay. But just a little." She nudged him gently and then got to rummaging about in Jackson's cupboards.

"I'm sure there's something edible around here somewhere," she muttered with her head in the larder. "Want to get a fire going for me while I work? I think I saw some matches above the mantle."

Gabe chuckled. "Sure thing. One fire coming right up."

It took longer than it had any right to, but soon enough Sariah found enough ingredients to cook a meal. There were carrots, celery, some onions, plenty of water, and even a slab of cured bacon in the larder. She could make quite the hearty stew out of all of that.

She stole another glance at Gabe. He was standing hunched over the fireplace with some wadded paper in one hand and a match in the other, trying to figure out how to make it all work.

Poor thing, she thought. Doesn't even know how to light a real fire.

She walked over and took the goods out of his hands. Their hands touched for a moment and a small tingle shot through her body. His warm hands felt good on a cold night like this. Too good.

Maybe it was the battle lust still coursing through her veins, but she was imagining a very different kind of battle taking place that night. One she'd thoroughly enjoy.

Sariah shook her head to clear it. "Here, let me get that going for you. Why don't you slice some vegetables? You seem to be pretty handy with a blade."

Gabe smiled at her. "If you think that was something, you should see me go to work against a real opponent." He waved a hand dismissively. "Those guards weren't even a challenge."

"Mm, I bet." She envisioned him fighting a really tough sword battle, his muscles bulging and his skin glistening with sweat. It was a good image.

Then she returned her attention to the fire. It wasn't going to get lit this way. Within a few moments, she had a small blaze going nice and strong. She put a couple of logs onto the budding flame and then got a pot and filled it with water.

Sariah looked at Gabe. He was slicing through the vegetables like a pro. A smile came to her lips again and she found herself blushing for no reason she could think of.

"Hey!" she called over to him.

Gabe's head perked up and he stared straight at her. "What's up?"

"Mind helping me get this pot on the fire?" She pointed to the giant pot full of water she was trying in vain to carry. It was heavier than it looked. In reality, she probably could have managed just fine on her own, but she wanted the excuse to be close to him.

Gabe put his knife down. "Certainly," he said, smiling at her. "Always happy to lend you a hand or two."

"Why thank you," she replied, batting her eyes.

He came over and picked up the handle to the pot.

Their hands touched again, and Sariah felt another hot sensation course through her.

I could get used to having a big, strong man like him around.

"How's it coming?" She asked him, craning her head toward the counter. "Almost ready?"

Gabe turned and looked at her with a sheepish grin. "How's what now?"

She pointed at the vegetables again. "The veggies, silly. How are they coming along? Is it time to put them in the water yet?"

Gabe chuckled a little bit. It only made him look more attractive. "Oh, that." He cleared his throat. "Um, it's almost ready. Let me go finish them."

He went back to the vegetables and she watched him work, mesmerized.

What am I doing? She shook her head to try and clear it. Do I really like him that much? I mean, this is Gabe we're talking about!

Still, somehow it felt right. Maybe it was the high of the recent victory getting to her, but right then she felt like she needed him in ways she'd never needed anyone before.

Gabe walked over and tossed the vegetables and the bacon into the pot. Sariah made sure they brushed up against each other again when he passed by her. She desperately wanted to feel his closeness.

"So, what now?" Gabe asked her.

An idea popped into her head, and she pushed it down. It wouldn't do to be that forward. "Umm..." she said. "Let me think about it."

Gabe flashed her another smile. "Okay, well I'm good with just about anything, you know."

Sariah nodded. She had another idea. It was silly, but she liked it. "Wait here. I'll be back in a few minutes." She rushed over to where their packs lay and grabbed something from them, then ran upstairs.

Gabe tapped his foot impatiently. Sariah had been upstairs for what felt like an hour, even if it had only been a few minutes.

What is that girl doing up there? he wondered. She could be so mysterious sometimes.

Of course, he liked that about her. He liked a lot of things about her. They had really started to grow close to each other lately. At least he thought so.

And when they'd touched tonight, it felt like fire. Or magic. Only a type of magic he'd never experienced.

Still, she was only sixteen. Almost seventeen. And he was twenty-two. Not a ton older, perhaps, but enough to make it a bit on the weird side.

Besides, she didn't know the truth about him. If she did there was no way she'd still be interested. She'd hate him for it.

What if she didn't hate me?

He shook his head to clear his thoughts. He was still high from the battle. The after-effects hadn't worn off, and he knew that could have an effect on other emotions, too. That was all this was. Just a quick battle-infused infatuation.

"Sorry," Sariah's voice called from the top of the stairs. "This thing is a pain to put on by yourself."

Gabe laughed to himself and shook his head. It was just like a girl to change before dinner. They were always thinking about their clothes.

He turned to look at her and stopped. She was absolutely stunning. She was wearing a long, flowing red dress that had a v-cut down the front and long sleeves that went almost all the way down to her hands. It was covered in lace and little sequins that sparkled in the low light of the house.

The dress was very form-fitting and accentuated her perfectly in all the right spots. She'd even taken the time to pin her hair into a bun so it wasn't spilling all over the place in sweaty, tangled knots.

In a word, she was beautiful.

"Wow," he said, not sure what else to say.

She beamed at him and started down the stairs, turning to and fro to let the fabric of the dress swish about. "Do you really like it?"

He looked her up and down once more. "You look...amazing."

A frown formed on her face and she waved a hand at him. "Aww, you're just saying that. My face is probably still horribly bruised from the battle. I look terrible."

Gabe shook his head. "No, I mean it." He reached up and brushed a tiny lock of hair out of her face. "You look fantastic."

She blushed and lowered her head slightly. Then in a rush, she grabbed his hand. "Here," she said, "you have to feel this fabric! It's so soft and silky!" She guided his hand to a non-beaded section of the dress near her abdomen.

He tried to jerk his hand away but relented quickly. Her touch felt good, and the fabric really was soft.

"You weren't kidding," he remarked, petting the fabric lightly. As he stroked it with his hand, little jolts of desire shot through him.

"Told you." She was beaming at him like an idiot.

Heat rose to his cheeks. It was too much. He withdrew his hand and backed away a half step. She looked disappointed at his abrupt departure, but he had no choice. If he wasn't careful, he would go too far.

Gabe lifted up an object with his other hand - a bottle of wine he'd found while rummaging about and waiting for Sariah to change.

"I found this in the priest's cupboards," he offered. "Want some while we wait for dinner?"

Sariah flashed him a quick smile. "I'd love some." She walked over to the couch in the center of the main room, sat down, and patted the cushion next to her. "Come sit next to me and we can share it and talk."

Gabe sighed. So much for stalling. He supposed sitting and talking wouldn't hurt. What kind of trouble could they get into on the couch, anyway?

He sat down next to her while also staying as far away as possible without making it look too awkward. It was a delicate balance, to be sure. One he wasn't altogether certain he'd pulled off.

Gabe uncorked the bottle with one deft motion of his hands and took a swig. The liquid burned on the way down. This stuff was stronger than what he was used to. He eyed the bottle strangely.

Just what does this priest get into in this little town, anyway?

He shook his head. It didn't really matter.

Sariah was holding her hand out for the bottle expectantly. He wondered for a moment if it was safe to give such a strong elixir to her, then shrugged and did it anyway.

A swig or two wouldn't hurt anyone.

Sariah stared down at the near-empty bottle of wine in her hands, then back up at Gabriel. She absent-mindedly bit her lip.

He sure did look good.

So far, this little quasi-date of hers was going pretty well. She'd managed not to burn dinner yet, he'd complimented her on her clothing, and they'd had a pretty pleasant conversation over a bottle of wine for the last half hour or so.

She stared at him with dreamy eyes. She was getting a bit of a buzz from the alcohol.

Was this what being drunk felt like? she wondered. She didn't know. Strong alcohol was a luxury for most in Chatwick, and as poor as she'd been growing up, she'd only tasted the stuff a handful of times.

Sariah took another sip of the wine. It was bitter, but with a tinge of sweetness. She didn't get the appeal of the stuff.

"You never did tell me about your days as a Dusk Raven," she said. Then she frowned and bit her lip again.

What am I doing? Why am I bringing up stupid questions like that at a time like this?

Gabe let out one of his signature sighs. She gave him another smile and waved her hand. "It's okay, you don't have to answer that. I shouldn't have asked."

He smiled back at her and nodded.

Sariah reached out a hand and stroked Gabe's chin. It was a little rough from some fresh stubble, but also strong and warm to the touch.

"You look nice, too, you know," she told him.

Gabe picked up her hand and moved it off of him very gently. "I think maybe you've had too much wine, Sariah," he said in an all-too-serious tone.

She frowned at him. "Nonsense! I'm fine!" She reached out with one finger and bonked him lightly on the nose with the tip of it. "Maybe it's you that's had too much."

A giggle escaped her lips and she clapped her hand over her mouth. She looked at him with a sheepish grin.

Gabe shook his head at her. "Yeah, time to put the wine away." He took the bottle from her.

Sariah was about to argue when an awful scent assaulted her nostrils. It was coming from over her shoulder. She turned to see smoke coming from inside the stew pot, and not the good kind, either.

"Scheisse!" she swore. She'd managed to burn the food again, after all.

Instinctively, she shot up to put out the burning hot pot, but Gabe forced her down.

"Hey," he said calmly.

"But! The food!" She motioned toward the pot with one of her hands.

Gabe glanced at the pot then back at her. "It's okay. I wasn't that hungry anyway."

Sariah felt heat rising to her cheeks. She blushed and lowered her gaze. "I should have known better than to try to make you dinner. I always burn the food," she said in a defeated tone.

Gabe took her chin in his hand and lifted it until they were looking into each other's eyes. "It's okay," he said again. "I mean it."

But Sariah wasn't paying attention to his words anymore. She felt a surge of desire come up from within her. It was overwhelming. She stared deep into his eyes and found solace there unlike any she'd ever known.

Gabe reached forward with his head, then his lips puckered. She parted her lips slightly and brought her mouth up to meet his.

They kissed for only a moment, but it was the most amazing thing Sariah had ever experienced. It was like sunshine, fireworks, and finding home all at the same time. Then it was over.

He pulled away from her almost as quickly as he'd moved in. He looked away and held his head in his hands. "I'm sorry," he muttered.

Sariah frowned at him. "For what?"

He was shaking his head. "I had no right to -"

She grabbed him. "It's not like I wasn't willing!" She tried to pull his hands away from his face and make him look at her, but he wouldn't budge.

Gabe sighed. "You wouldn't understand. I...I'm sorry." He got up off the couch and started to walk away.

Sariah groaned. "Come back, Gabe!" she whined. "It's okay, we don't even have to talk about it. We can pretend it didn't happen. Please?" She got up as well, then and started walking toward him, but didn't get very far.

At that exact moment, the door to Jackson's home came crashing open. Harvey burst through, face beaming with one of his signature dopey grins.

"Sariah! Gabe! I'm back!" he shouted. "Did you miss me?"

CHAPTER FOURTEEN

Sariah brought her blade up to parry the blow just in time. She let out an inward sigh of relief and readied her own attack.

That was a close one, she thought.

She went for a wild swing toward Harvey's middle. He was ready for her and batted away her thrust like it wasn't even there.

Her face contorted into a grimace and she tried another angle but met with similar success. There was no doubt about it. Harvey was a good opponent for her.

She was getting better, though. Last night, she'd managed to get past his defenses and give him a tiny nick on one of his cheeks. So far, though, today she'd had no such luck.

Growling, she tried for a low thrust. This one looked like it would connect for a half-second, then Harvey managed to parry that blow as well.

She had an idea. She pushed upward with her blade,

then halfway up she changed direction and went for Harvey's sword arm.

She heard him wince in pain as her blade connected with the flesh of his arm for a brief second.

"Hold!" Harvey shouted. It was their agreed-upon stop word.

Sariah nodded and dropped her blade. She smiled at him. "I got you again this time."

Harvey nodded and grinned at her. "Your skills are definitely improving. I'm proud of you."

He held up his wounded arm to inspect it. She eyed it critically. There was a scratch there that was maybe an inch long.

"Looks like I got you pretty good, too," she insisted. She grabbed his arm. "Here, let me help you."

Harvey withdrew the injured appendage and waved dismissively with the other one. "Don't worry about it. Nothing Gabe can't fix."

Sariah rolled her eyes at the mention of Gabe's name. Harvey adored him like always, but ever since that night in Chatwick, things hadn't been the same for her.

In her mind's eye, she relived the moments of that night. Things had started out so well until they'd shared that fateful kiss.

From then on, it had gone downhill and fast. He'd clammed up since, barely even talking to her unless he absolutely had to. It was like the early days of their relationship all over again.

What is it with guys and their stupid feelings, anyway? She didn't know if it was something wrong with her.

She shook her head. That line of thinking had gotten

her nowhere over the last two weeks. It wouldn't do her any good to go back to it now.

The very next morning Gabe had decided they should go back to Stratton to be near the Dusk Raven stronghold so they could plan their next attack.

Sariah had been good with that, at first, but they'd been back in Stratton for a week now and they hadn't done any planning. Only more training, both magical and physical.

Not that she minded the training. Her battle with Severin had proved she still had a lot to learn about handling her own in a fight.

Sariah looked at Harvey's wound again. She scoffed at him. "You're going to bother Gabe to heal that tiny little scratch?" She squinted at the mark on his arm.

Harvey flashed her one of his dopey grins. "And why not?"

She chuckled, then looked him up and down. "Wimp."

Harvey looked at his wound, then back at her with a sheepish expression on his face. "Am not," he insisted.

Sariah smiled. "Totally a wimp. Can't even handle a tiny little scar." She pressed the issue a little further. "What's wrong, can't handle the fact you got beat by a woman?"

Harvey scowled at her. "What? You know I don't care about that sort of thing!"

She nodded. "Uh-huh. Sure, you don't."

He rubbed his skin next to the wound. "Ugh."

"Aww, poor wittle Harvey," Sariah said in a motherly tone. "He got his big bad feelers hurt by a mean wittle girl. Can't even handle a teeny weeny wittle scratch."

Harvey rolled his eyes. "It's not that!" he fired back. Then, in a softer tone, he added, "It just itches a little is all."

Sariah's thoughts returned to Gabe. On the trip back and once or twice since she'd tried her best to corner Gabe and continue their conversation from their ill-fated "date night," as she called it, but to no avail. Harvey pretty much never left them alone, and when she did get a moment's peace, Gabe would clam up.

The problem was obvious to her - their emotions had been too compromised in Chatwick. They were still coming off a battle high and she had been a little drunk. Poor Gabe had undoubtedly felt like he was taking advantage of her heightened emotions. It was no wonder he'd backed away.

She intended to get things back on track. All she needed was a plan and a way to get him alone for a bit away from Harvey and everything else. Looking at Harvey's arm, a thought came to her about how to do it.

Sariah looked at the scratch again with a critical eye. She ran a finger around the edge of it and made a sour expression with her lips. "Ew. I think you might be right. It might be infected."

Harvey gulped loudly. "Really?" he asked. There was a hint of fear in his eyes.

She shrugged. "It's possible. Hard to say for sure. But better safe than sorry."

He nodded. "Right. I'll go get Gabe."

She put her hand on his chest to stop him. "You really think he's going to want to be bothered over that tiny thing? You know it's his meditation time. You'd never live it down, ruining his meditation over a tiny little scratch."

"Yeah," Harvey admitted. He rubbed his chin. "You might be right. He'd be in a foul mood if this wound turned out to be nothing and his meditation hour was wasted."

Sariah nodded. "Mm-hm. Very foul."

Harvey looked at her. "What should we do, then?"

"You stay here. I'll go fetch some salve from the market for that wound of yours."

Harvey gave her a curt nod. "Sound plan. Just hurry back, will you? It really does itch something fierce."

She giggled as she started walking away. "Of course!"

"Don't tell Gabe about what happened!" he shouted after her.

"Wouldn't dream of it!"

A big smile crept upon her lips. Phase one complete. On to phase two.

Sariah gave Gabe's door a hard, swift knock. She hadn't been lying about this being his meditation time, and it really was a pain to get his attention during it.

Her mind was consumed with her "master plan." With how scared Harvey had looked over that tiny scratch, he wasn't likely to leave the training room until well after nightfall in order to not risk getting sick.

It was cruel in a way, but also genius. Besides, she thought, he brought it on himself by insisting that I never go off alone.

Sariah rolled her eyes and knocked on the door again, even louder. She started tapping her foot impatiently. She didn't want to squander this time waiting for Gabe to even notice her.

A moment later, she heard a groan and the sound of someone moving about. She heard Bear barking at Gabe, and Gabe shushing him.

She mentally chuckled as she imagined what their conversations were like. Bear was a fun companion. In some ways far superior to her human ones. Or at the very least far less broody.

The door to Gabe's room creaked and opened just a crack. "Who is it?" Gabe's voice asked from within.

Sariah gave the door a shove. Remarkably, it moved and Gabe was forced back half a step. He must not have been ready for her to move so fast.

Big softy, she thought with another chuckle.

"There you are!" Sariah said with a half scowl as she forced herself the rest of the way into the room. "I've been looking all over for you!"

She blinked a couple of times to let her eyes adjust. Gabe's room was darker than usual and it smelled a little smoky.

What does he do here during meditation times, anyway? She shook her head. It didn't matter.

"Me?" Gabe replied, pointing to himself. "What did you need me for, exactly?"

Sariah kept shaking her head. "It's Harvey. He's gone and injured himself during training."

Gabe straightened up and looked at Sariah. "Where is he? I'll take care of it right away."

She put her hand out. "He doesn't want any magical help for this one," she lied.

"He doesn't?" Gabe stared at her and blinked. "That's...odd."

She shook her head vigorously. "No sir. Said he 'didn't want to upset my sensibilities' or some nonsense. As if I even care anymore." She sighed. "He really is stubborn and pig-headed sometimes, you know."

"That sounds just like Harvey. He can be such an idiot sometimes."

Sariah smiled. "Don't I know it." She looked around. "I didn't want to bother you about it, but I'm worried it might be infected."

He rubbed his chin. "Well, what do you want to do about it?"

She shrugged. "Oh, I don't know. I thought maybe we could go to Market Square and pick up some salve for it? Something he wouldn't object to." She paused for a moment. "I'm only thinking of Harvey."

Gabe sighed. "Oh, of course. It's only for Harvey." He pulled on his face again. He looked tired. After a moment, he agreed. "All right, let's get going."

She smiled back at him. "I was hoping you'd say that."

Market Square was busy this time of day. It was near noon and the sun was beating down, making everyone just a little uncomfortable in the crowded space.

Sariah looked at Gabe and frowned. He was still acting distant. She had to think of some way to get him to open up or her love life would be doomed to remain barren forever.

She looked at the crowds and started to feel claustrophobic. Even though she'd been in Stratton for some time now, she hadn't gone to market square that often, and today was a particularly busy day at the market.

Almost instinctively, she grabbed Gabe's hand. He looked at her strangely but said nothing.

"Hold my hand," she asked him. "I don't want to get separated."

He gave her a weak smile but still said nothing. Still, at least he didn't let go. It was a start.

Sariah decided to try and be a bit more forward. "We're alone now, you know," she said. "Just the two of us. No Harvey."

He nodded. "Yep."

Sariah furrowed her brow. One-word answers weren't going to cut it. She needed more from him.

"You know, if there was anything you wanted to say, or...or do...or, you know, you could do it," she offered.

Gabe turned and looked at her. The two stopped walking. Waves of people crashed about them and moaned, but in that moment Sariah felt like it was just the two of them in the entire world.

His face softened. "Sariah, I..."

She smiled up at him. "Yes?"

He let out a deep, long sigh. This time, she didn't mind it. "I'm sorry I've been so..."

"Distant?" she finished for him.

His eyes looked lost in thought for a moment. "Yes, I think that's the term."

Sariah reached up and touched his cheek. It was as rough and rugged as she remembered from that night in Chatwick, and there was still a hint of fire in his touch. "It's okay, you know."

Gabe flashed her another weak smile. He took hold of her other hand. "No, it's not. I shouldn't have taken advantage of you like that."

She shook her head. "Is that what you think? It wasn't like that. I wanted it, too."

He looked around shifty-eyed like he was expecting something to pounce out of the crowd and attack them. "Look, you're young and I, well..."

Sariah groaned. Without thinking, she leaned up and planted a kiss on his lips. It was quick and a bit rough, not sweet like the last time, but it still left her feeling good.

Gabe looked stunned. For a moment, he looked at her like she'd grown two heads. Then finally, his lips turned upward into a smile.

"Now that wasn't so bad, was it?" she said, grinning at him.

He looked at her and past her at the same time. "I guess not." He sighed again. "You're not mad at me, then?"

Sariah laughed. "No. Not anymore."

Gabe smiled at her and squeezed her hand. "You have no idea how happy I am to hear you say that." He shifted on his feet. "Now, let's go get that salve for Harvey, shall we?"

She nodded. Then her heart dropped. She'd almost forgotten about her cover story. The medicine stall was just up ahead, and she wasn't ready for their little bit of alone time to be over just yet. She needed another diversion.

An idea came to her. It was a long shot, but it might work. She bit her lip and went with it.

"Come with me," she insisted, pulling on Gabe's hand.

Gabe chuckled. "What are you doing?" he asked. "The medicine stall is that way." He pointed behind him.

"There's something I want you to see first. Just come with me. Please?" She looked at him with pleading in her eyes.

He sighed again and shook his head. "All right," he said slowly.

Sariah led him by the hand toward the rear portion of Market Square. She knew just where she was headed.

Moving with purpose as they were, they made their way through the crowds in record time. She held onto Gabe's hand the whole time. Not because she was afraid of getting separated, but because she didn't want to let go yet. It was nice. She could get used to this.

Before long, they reached their destination. Sariah looked at the old dress merchant's stall and smiled. Good, she thought. It's still here.

Sariah turned to Gabe. "There's someone I'd like you to meet," she said.

Gabe looked at her confused, then looked at the stall in front of them. "Dresses? You want another dress?" There was a hint of distaste in his voice.

She rolled her eyes. "No, silly. Just come on." She pulled on his arm and practically forced him into the tent.

Gabe looked around the tent and a vague look of recognition passed across his eyes. "Is this?"

Sariah nodded. "Yep." She looked around and spotted the old dress merchant hunched over a pile of fabrics.

Her face brightened at the sight of the old woman. "Valerie!" she called out. "There's someone here I'd like you to meet!"

The old woman turned. "Sariah?" she said with hesitation. "Is that you?"

Sariah nodded. "It is indeed."

Valerie reached out and hugged her warmly. "I'm so glad you're safe. Does that mean your little mission was a success?"

She nodded again. "Mm-hm. All thanks to you."

Valerie waved her off. "Oh, you're too kind." Her attention shifted to Gabe. The dress merchant's eyes narrowed and her face darkened, but Sariah didn't notice. "And who is this with you?" The old woman held out a hand to Gabe.

Sariah turned and pushed Gabe forward. "This is Gabe. He's my...my friend." She motioned from Gabe to Valerie and back again. "Gabe, this is Valerie. She made me feel at home when we first got here. And she sewed that dress you like so much."

Gabe took Valerie's offered hand and shook it. "So, you're the dressmaker I've heard so much about," he said.

Valerie tilted her head just slightly. "Aye, dearie. Nice to meet you." She withdrew her hand quickly.

"Well, I must thank you," Gabe told her. He pulled on his shirt. "These clothes have really held up well."

The old woman tilted her head again. "I'd expect nothing less."

Sariah looked between the two and was dumbfounded. These were two of her favorite people in the world at the moment, but they didn't seem to be getting along like she'd hoped.

What was wrong?

She didn't have long to ponder it. Gabe looked around and started to back away. He turned his attention back to

Sariah. "We should really go get that salve, now," he said coolly.

Sariah nodded at him. "Okay." She turned to face Valerie. "I'll come back to see you soon, okay?"

Valerie nodded once.

Sariah turned to leave with Gabe, but Valerie shot out her hand and grabbed her by the arm. "Actually, Sariah, why don't you stay a moment. I've got a new fabric I'd love to show you." She looked at Gabe. "I won't keep her long. Women's stuff, you understand."

"Sure, I get it." He looked at Sariah. "I'll wait for you over at the medicine stall, okay?"

Sariah nodded. "Okay." She gave his hand another squeeze. "See you soon."

Gabe winked at her and walked away slowly. She smiled at him the whole time he was leaving.

When he was gone, she turned to look at Valerie. "Where's this fabric you want me to-"

She didn't finish her sentence. Valerie was giving her a look that said she was scared or nervous. Whatever the older woman wanted to talk to her about, it obviously wasn't fabric.

"What's wrong?" Her smile quickly faded into a frown.

Valerie's eyes darted around like she was scanning Market Square beyond for signs of danger. Then she inched forward and pulled Sariah in extra close, to the point where her lips were practically touching her ear.

The old woman opened her mouth and warm, hot air assaulted Sariah's ears, but she didn't back away.

Sariah could feel the other woman's lips trembling in

fear. Her stomach started to churn and for a moment she regretted eating seconds at breakfast.

In a voice barely louder than a whisper, Valerie finally uttered a few choice words. "Run," she whispered. "Run away as fast as you can."

CHAPTER FIFTEEN

Gabe tapped his foot impatiently while he waited. He'd bought the damn salve for Harvey several minutes ago and now he was waiting for Sariah to come back to him.

He thought back to the events of earlier that day and of the night they'd shared in Chatwick before Harvey had interrupted them.

What's keeping Sariah? he wondered. Surely looking at fabrics can't take that long.

At first, he'd thought Harvey's interruption in Chatwick had been a good thing. He had been making a right fool of himself in front of an impressionable young girl, and about to make a giant mistake. But now, after today? He wasn't so sure anymore.

Today was like something out of a daydream. Sariah liked him. Not just as a mentor, but actually liked him. People like him didn't deserve a girl like that to like them. Not really. She was good and wholesome and wonderful in all the right ways. And he? He was a liar, and an overall bad person.

He shook his head. No, fates like this weren't meant for people like him. It was more than he could ever hope for, being on the path that he was on. Yet here he was, living this strange, wondrous dream.

Gabe whistled a happy tune softly to himself. Things were going right for once. In the mood he was in, anything was possible. He just had to wait for Sariah to get back so he could talk to her again. Really talk to her. About everything this time.

Under any other circumstances, he wouldn't even consider such a step. But Sariah was different. She liked him and trusted him in ways no one else ever had. That kind of trust deserved to be rewarded. She deserved to know the truth he'd been hiding all this time.

It's time, he thought. Time to let someone...no, time to let her in. Time to realize my wildest dreams.

If only she'd show up. He tapped his foot again and checked the position of the sun. It was getting into the afternoon now.

What is taking her so long?

Just then, he caught someone approaching his location. His heart skipped a beat and a lump formed in his throat. He was ready to take this step, he was sure of it.

Sariah pulled her head away from Valerie and looked at the old woman like she'd grown another head. "I'm sorry?" she said slowly.

Valerie's eyes still had fear in them. She wet her cracked

lips and spoke again, a little firmer this time. "You need to run, dearie. As far and as fast as you can."

Sariah blinked and shook her head. She was starting to grow scared herself. "You're not making any sense."

The older woman took a half step toward her to close the distance. She put one of her hands on Sariah's shoulder, but she shirked it off.

"Listen to me, dearie. You don't know quite what you've gotten yourself into, but I do."

"What's that even supposed to mean?" Sariah moaned. She was talking quite loudly, loud enough that people outside the booth could likely hear.

Valerie put a hand to her lips. "Shh, quiet down please. Please. For your own good." There was a look of urgency in her eyes.

Sariah wasn't quite sure what to think. The dress merchant was obviously afraid for her very life. But why? It didn't make any sense. None of this made any sense. Her behavior had been so strange.

"What's going on?" Sariah demanded in a quieter tone. "Please, tell me what's going on here. You've been acting cagey since I got here."

The dress merchant took a step back and looked at her. She nodded once and pulled on her face. "You're right," she replied. "You're right. I'm skipping ahead a bit. You deserve a full explanation. It's just...that man."

"That man?" Sariah looked over her shoulder and then back at Valerie. She pointed behind her. "You don't mean? Gabriel?"

Valerie nodded slowly. The color had drained

completely from her face. She licked her lips again to wet them. "Yes, dearie. That's the one."

She looked at the old woman cross-eyed. "What's wrong with Gabe?"

The older woman did a double take. "You have a nick-name for that wretched human?" she said in an exasper-ated tone. She looked at the sky for a second and placed one hand on her hip and the other under her chin. "This is far worse than I thought."

Sariah shook her head. "What? What's so bad? Just please, tell me!"

Valerie looked at her again, this time with a hint of pity in her eyes. "Tell me, sweet Sariah. How long have you known this...Gabriel? When did you meet him?"

She let out a nervous laugh. "Gabe? I met him ages ago. He's the one who brought me here to begin with."

The dress merchant shook her head slowly. She patted one of Sariah's shoulders. "Oh, you poor thing. You've been misled for so long. No wonder it's hard to see the light."

Sariah scoffed. "Look, I like you Valerie and I'm eter-nally grateful for the help you gave me all those weeks ago, but unless you start making sense real fast, I'm afraid I'm going to have to go." She started to turn around to go back to her friends.

Valerie's eyes grew wide and she shot out her hand and grabbed Sariah by the arm. The move was forceful this time and a wave of pain shot up Sariah's arm. "No!" she insisted. "Please, just hear me out first."

She looked at the older woman intently. That sense of fear and foreboding was back. She put her hand on

Valerie's hand and squeezed it gently. "Fine, but let go of me. That hurts."

The dress merchant withdrew her hand quickly. "I'm sorry, dearie," she said quickly. "Truly, I am."

Sariah shook her arm a few times. It still stung, but it didn't look like there would be any bruises or anything. She returned her attention to the old woman. "Now talk."

Valerie's eyes rolled up for a second, then she looked back at Sariah. The old woman was tapping her foot nervously. "Where to start, where to start..."

"How about somewhere that makes sense."

The old woman nodded at her. "Of course." She smoothed out the fabric of her dress and stood up tall. "Look, I don't know what that...Gabriel person has told you, but he's not a safe man. He's very dangerous."

Sariah rolled her eyes. "Of course, he's dangerous! He's a master magician and swordsman. But he's never hurt me."

Valerie shook her head. "You misunderstand, dearie. He's...he's a known Dusk Raven, and not just any rank and file member, either."

Sariah burst out laughing. She didn't know what she'd expected to hear, but it wasn't that. "Is that all?" she replied. "It's okay, I know about his past."

The older woman shook her head again. "I'm serious, dearie. He's a bad person. He's with the group that killed your parents."

She waved the older woman off. "He told me all about it ages ago. How he used to be with them. He's not any longer, though. He's changed."

"Oh, you poor thing," Valerie said with a sigh. "Is that what he told you?"

Sariah let out another nervous laugh. "Of course. What else is there to tell?"

The older woman placed a gentle hand on her shoulder again. That look of pity was back. "It was a lie, I'm afraid. I can assure you, he is very much still a Dusk Raven. One of the Master's top generals, in fact."

She pushed the old woman's hand off her and scowled at her. Blood rushed to her cheeks. "What would you know anyway? I've been with him these last few months. He's far too kind and gentle to be a bad guy."

Valerie's look changed to one of concern. "Listen, dearie. I know what I'm talking about. I'm partnered with a faction known as the Eagle's Claw - a group that's been fighting against the Dusk Ravens. Good people who are trying to free this land of their oppressive regime." She looked Sariah up and down. "How else do you think I knew where their base was?"

That struck a nerve with her. It was true, the old woman had known just where to find the Dusk Ravens earlier. It hadn't seemed odd at the time, but now she had to wonder.

She looked at Valerie again. Part of her wanted to run away and live out her life like this conversation had never happened, but the rest of her wanted to stay and listen.

The latter part eventually won. She nodded her head slowly. "Tell me, then, Valerie. How do you know he's still one of them? What proof do you have?"

Valerie laid her hands bare. "Just my word, dearie. People like him don't leave witnesses to their deeds."

Sariah frowned. She had been stupid to trust this merchant over Gabe. She knew Gabe. Trusted him.

"I thought so," she said slowly. "I think I'll go now." She turned and started walking out of the booth.

"No, wait!" Valerie shouted. She reached forward and grabbed hold of Sariah's shirt and wouldn't let go. "Please! I don't want to see the same thing that happened to Jakob happen to you, too!"

Sariah's heart froze and a knot of fear formed in her gut. She'd heard that name before. It was the name of Gabe's old mentor.

He wasn't dead. He'd gone off on a pilgrimage.

She turned slowly. "What did you just say?"

Valerie looked up at her. "I don't want to see you end up dead, dearie. Like all the rest have before you."

She blinked her eyes in disbelief. "Did you say Jakob is dead?"

The old woman bobbed her head. "Aye, dearie. Slain by the hand of his student when he wouldn't go over to his side." She made some strange symbol like a cross with her hands in front of her chest. "Jakob was one of our best men."

"No, that can't be." Sariah shook her head. "Gabe told me Jakob had gone on a pilgrimage. You must be mistaken."

Valerie gave her that pitying look again. "I wish I were, dearie, but it's true. The man who calls himself Gabriel is a monster. He's not safe. If you're not careful, you'll be next in line."

Her heart sank further. Could any of this be true?

Impossible! she thought. I know Gabe. He wouldn't do

such things. Still, she was starting to doubt. He had disappeared a few times with not much to show for it, and he did seem to know a lot about the Dusk Ravens' current plans. If he were with them, then why help her take them out?

She gave the old woman a weak smile. "Look, I appreciate the warning, and maybe Gabe was like that once, but he's changed. I promise."

The dress merchant sighed. "Very well, dearie. If you ever change your mind, my people have a base three days southeast of here. It's a walled city called Talon's Reach. You can't miss it. Approach the guards and tell them 'the eagle has risen over the hills.' They'll know what to do."

Sariah blinked a few times and looked at Valerie one last time. That look of pity was still there, even stronger than before.

Was the dress merchant right? She wanted to say no, but she couldn't quite be sure. It nagged at her. She gave the old woman a weak smile. "Gee, thanks I guess," she responded. Then she turned and left the stall as quickly as she could.

***

Gabe squinted at the form walking toward him. It was a little too big to be Sariah. Soon enough, it came into focus. It was Harvey, with Bear in tow.

Gabe wondered what he was doing out here.

He frowned at the duo. They were bounding their way over to him happily enough, but he wasn't equally happy to see them.

Ugh, he thought. I'll never get Sariah to myself as long as that kid's around. He rolled his eyes.

Harvey waved to him. Reluctantly, he waved back and gave the kid a half-smile.

"Ho!" Harvey called out to him. Bear let out a sharp bark.

Gabe made a beckoning motion with his hand. "Harvey. Bear. Come here. What brings you out here?" His eyes trailed to a tiny scratch on Harvey's arm. "I thought Sariah said you were injured?"

Harvey chuckled. "What? This little scratch?" He pointed to the small wound on his arm and shrugged. "It's nothing."

Gabe squinted to look at it. "Yeah, I can see that. I thought she said it was infected or something. But how could that be infected?"

The younger man waved him off with a hand. "Pfft. She told me the same thing, but it's fine, I swear. Barely even hurts."

Gabe nodded. "That's good."

Harvey shook his head. "I think Sariah was just trying to get some time by herself. It's been crowded around here lately, don't you think?"

Gabe let out a weak laugh. "You can say that again." He eyed the kid. "So, why'd you come out here then?"

Harvey shrugged his shoulders again. "I thought she'd be out here, you know, in the market. What about you? Why are you here?"

"Sariah wanted me to see some dress or something," Gabe lied. He quickly shuffled the jar of salve in his hands into one of his pockets. "I think she wanted me to buy it for her. She's trying it on now."

Harvey nodded. "That's fair. Why are you out here and not there?"

Gabe shrugged. "She wanted her privacy dressing."

The two looked at each other uncomfortably for a moment saying nothing. Gabe let a slight frown escape his lips. He'd really been hoping he'd get some more time alone with Sariah. Now he'd have to find another way to make that happen.

He didn't get long to think about it, though, because a moment later Sariah came into view.

"How was the dress?" Gabe asked her.

Sariah looked up at him, but her eyes looked strange. Distracted, and like something was off.

"Hmm?" she asked like she was in a daze. "Oh, yes, the dress. It was okay. Hard pass from me." She smiled at him, but the smile was weak.

Gabe nodded and smiled back at her, but inwardly his thoughts were racing. Something was wrong, he could tell. It was like she'd come back from the dress merchant a completely different person.

"Everything okay?" he asked.

Sariah looked at him. "Of course, why wouldn't it be?" She flicked a strand of hair out of her face.

Gabe's heart sank. Something was up, all right and with Harvey here, there was no way he'd get to the bottom of it. He'd have to figure something out.

"Let's get back to The Dragonfly," he suggested. "You all must be exhausted after the day's training. He offered her his hand, but she didn't accept it. It was like she didn't even notice it was there.

"Sure," she replied in a wooden voice. "Sounds great."

Harvey furrowed his brow and looked at Sariah. They'd been back at The Dragonfly for well over an hour and the girl hadn't spoken a single word the entire time. It wasn't like her.

She hadn't touched her dinner, either. That was definitely unusual. If there was one thing he could count on with Sariah, it was her appetite.

Something was definitely going on, but he had no idea what it could be. Was she feeling bad about injuring him in training earlier today? It wasn't like her to be sullen over something so trivial, but it was possible.

He sat down on the bed next to her. His motion seemed to break her from whatever trance-like state she was in and she turned to look at him, giving him a weak smile.

Harvey gave her one of his big, dopey grins in return, but it didn't garner any reaction.

"You okay?" he asked her.

Her eyes looked red and puffy like she'd been crying, but why was anyone's guess. For a moment, it looked like she was going to say something, but instead she turned her head and remained silent.

He put his hand on her chin and pulled her face toward him again. "Hey," he said softly. "You know, whatever it is, you can tell me, okay? We're friends. I can take anything."

She gave him a half-smile and patted him once on the

chest. Her gaze lowered and she let out a soft sigh. "Harvey?" she uttered in a light tone.

Harvey's eyes lit up. "Yes?"

Sariah turned her head away from him again. "It's nothing," she insisted. "Sorry I bothered you."

"Hey!" Harvey repeated, annoyed this time. "You are not bothering me. Get that thought out of your head this instant!"

"What happened to you?" He furrowed his brow. She was definitely in a bad spot.

"I mean it," he continued. "Whatever's bothering you, you can always come to me. I'm here for you, Sariah. I'll always be here for you."

Her eyes got a little brighter. "Harvey?"

"Yes?" His features softened.

"I don't want to talk about it," she blurted out at last.

"Ugh!" he groaned. He rolled his eyes and threw up his hands. "Come on, Sariah! I can tell something's wrong! Just, please, let me know what's going on in that head of yours!"

Sariah kept looking at him. At one point she bit her lip and rocked back and forth like she was dying to say something, but then she just turned her head again and looked away.

Harvey put a hand gently on her shoulder. "Is it Gabe?" he asked. The two of them had been acting odd toward each other lately. "Did something happen with Gabe?"

Sariah shook her head violently and started to make a slight sobbing sound.

Now he knew something was really wrong. It wasn't like Sariah to cry. She'd barely even cried when her parents had died. She'd been numb and angry more than anything. If she had been brought to tears, it was something serious.

He decided to press further. "Did Gabe say something mean to you?"

She shook her head again, softer than before.

Harvey thought hard. If he was honest with himself, Sariah had been acting off ever since the Battle of Chatwick. He'd chalked it up to after-effects of the fighting at first, but maybe it was more than that. She and Gabe had been in quite an interesting position when he'd walked in on them. Maybe something had happened.

He tried again. "Did Gabe do something to you?"

Sariah shook her head again.

"Back in Chatwick, I mean. Did he..." Heat rose to his cheeks. "Did he try to take advantage of you?"

She turned then. There was sadness in her eyes, but also a hint of anger. "Let's just please stop talking about Gabe, okay?" she insisted.

He shot up his hands in self-defense and backed away. "Sorry, I didn't mean to upset you."

Sariah sniffled once and her face softened. She rubbed her nose. "No, it's okay, I didn't mean to blow up at you like that."

Harvey gave her one of his dopey grins. This time she smiled. "Hey, it's okay. My fault, really. You did say you didn't want to talk about it."

"Yeah." She nodded at him and gave him a fake smile. "Sorry, I just...I can't right now, you know?"

"Sure," he replied. "I understand." In truth, it was anything but. He was dying to press her for more information, but he knew when to let things drop, and now was one of those times.

"I'm just tired, I think." She let out a big yawn. "Been a long day and all, you know?"

"Yeah, I get it. I'm a little tired myself."

"We can talk tomorrow, okay?" Sariah offered.

"Okay, sounds good." He got up and walked over to his bed. About halfway there, he turned back. "Are you sure you don't want me to go beat up Gabe for you?"

She shot him an icy glare. "No!" she insisted. "No, please don't do anything with Gabe! At least, not tonight," she added in a softer tone. "Promise me."

Harvey cocked his head and gave her a sideways glance. It was a very odd thing for her to make him promise. Now he was even more worried. There was something there he couldn't quite place. Fear, maybe. But of what?

"Sure thing, Sariah. Whatever you say." He flashed her one more grin. "Sorry for bringing it up."

"I'm sorry," she replied, wiping her nose again. "Seems I'm a bit of a mess tonight."

He waved her off with a hand. "It's okay. You've had a rough couple of weeks. Why don't we both get some sleep, okay?"

She bobbed her head. "Okay."

Harvey walked over and blew out the candle in their shared room, then went over to his bed, laid down, and pretended to go to sleep.

Internally, his mind was racing trying to figure out what had happened to Sariah to make her respond the way she had tonight. For a moment, he wished he was better at mental magic. He could read her mind to get the answers he sought.

He sighed. Even if he could do it, he knew he'd never betray Sariah's trust like that. He'd have to wait for her to open up on her own.

Until then, he'd just have to do everything he could to make sure she felt as safe as he could make her.

The young man laid his head on the pillow and turned his head so he could see Sariah clearly. One thing was for certain, he wasn't going to sleep tonight. Sariah needed him. That much was obvious. She could wake up at any time and be ready and willing to talk.

He'd always tried to be there for her, and though he'd failed several times, this time he'd make sure of it. Even if it meant staying up all night.

CHAPTER SIXTEEN

Sariah moaned softly to herself. She was lying in bed, thinking about the events of the previous day, wondering if Valerie had been honest with her, and if so, what that meant for her relationship with Gabe.

Her head was spinning, and she needed some time and space to get some clarity. There was one glaring issue confronting her - Harvey.

She turned her head ever so slightly to glance in his direction. Even in the darkness, she could tell he wasn't really sleeping. He did this thing with his eyes when he pretended to sleep where he kept one eye half-open so he didn't miss anything.

It was something he'd done ever since they were kids, and he was for sure doing it now.

Sariah sighed. He meant well, she knew. He only wanted to help her. But she didn't want his help right now. She wanted answers.

No, not wanted answers - needed them. Harvey wouldn't have them. If she started talking to Harvey about all of it now, she could imagine what would happen. They'd get into a fight and argue, then Harvey would sulk, and neither of them would feel any better at the end.

It was no use. Harvey liked Gabe. Adored him, even. Hell, she still did, even if he wasn't all he was cracked up to be. There was no way Harvey would believe the dress merchant over Gabe. He wouldn't agree to her current plan.

But he didn't know Valerie the way Sariah did and hadn't heard what she'd said and the fear in her eyes as she'd said it.

There was a kernel of truth in her words, at the very least. One Sariah was determined to find on her own, without potentially wrecking another relationship. To do that, she'd have to strike out on her own until this sordid mess was over.

What should I do about Harvey, then? she wondered. Would he be safe here, if Gabe was as bad as all that?

She bit her lip. Gabe had always been good to both of them from the start. Surely, he wouldn't hurt Harvey over her disappearance. She shook her head. It didn't fit with what she knew about him.

On top of that, Harvey was far from helpless. He could look out for himself.

He should be safe enough, she decided. Once she had settled the whole matter, it would be water under the bridge, and just a big misunderstanding.

Now all she had to do was find a way to get past him.

A thought came to her then, unbidden. She could use magic to put him to sleep. She'd seen Gabe do it a time or two back when Harvey had been injured after his kidnapping and had trouble going to sleep normally. It seemed like a simple enough trick, even if she'd never used it before herself.

She wasn't sure she could use magic against a friend without his knowledge. It felt icky and wrong, like something a Dusk Raven would do.

A chill ran up and down her spine and she wanted to retch. She needed time by herself, and she didn't see another way of achieving it.

Sariah closed her eyes and thought about the words of a lullaby. She hummed them softly to herself to help with her concentration and tried to will Harvey to go to sleep.

Nothing happened for a few minutes, but soon enough, she could hear the man snoring. She decided to risk it and take a look. Slowly, she shuffled around in her bed until she was facing him. She tried to make it look like she was just sleeping restlessly in case he was still awake.

She opened one eye and looked at Harvey fully. He was lying there with both eyes closed and making contented noises.

Her gambit had worked. A knot formed in her stomach, but she pushed it down and tried to forget it. She could worry about how her little act of subterfuge made her feel later when her head was clear. For now, she had a mission.

With Harvey out of the way, she got to work quickly. She packed her bag with a few supplies - enough to see her safe for a week or so - and put on a fresh set of clothes. She spotted her dirty clothes on the floor and decided to go ahead and fold them and place them neatly on the bed. She was already going to cause Harvey to have a small heart attack when he woke up. No sense in making him do extra labor on top of it.

She walked over to Harvey and took one last look at him. He looked peaceful, laying there like he was, contented and snoring. That feeling of disgust came up again and she pushed it back down once more.

He'll understand, she reasoned. Though she knew more than likely he would not. Still, she didn't want to take him with her. Not this time. There were some things a girl just had to do by herself.

She bent down and placed a gentle kiss on his forehead, then crept out of the room, trying hard not to make a sound. She had no way of knowing when her spell would wear off. After all, she still wasn't the best magician, but he didn't budge.

Once outside the room, she breathed a sigh of relief. Phase one of her plan was complete. Now came the harder part.

Sariah took a giant step forward and ended up planting her foot on something warm and furry. She made a slight yelping sound and looked down to see what it was.

Looking up at her was Bear. He gave her a yelp of his own and looked at her expectantly.

"Not now, Bear," she told the animal, giving him a pat on his head. "I need to do this by myself. You understand, don't you?"

She side-stepped the dog and went for the stairs. But Bear was fast, and he moved to block the way down the stairwell before she could make it there.

The young girl tilted her head to the side. "Come on, boy. You don't want any part of what I'm about to do." She nodded toward the door behind her. "Go back to your master. Please."

Bear let out a low growl and bared his teeth. He stood even firmer like he was getting ready to pounce.

Sariah rolled her eyes and groaned. "Fine," she said. "You can come, but don't wake the others. And don't complain to me later when you find out you don't like what we're doing."

The dog gave her an appreciative yip and licked her hand, then the two walked down the stairs together and outside The Dragonfly.

Sariah breathed another sigh of relief. She still had a lot of obstacles in her path, and a lot of answers to seek, but at least now she'd have a chance to pursue them.

Harvey woke to the sound of someone pounding on his bedroom door. The knocking sounded urgent and harried like the person had been doing it for a while.

The sun streaked through the window and played across his face, making it warm in spots. Slowly, he opened his eyes, then closed them again when the light glared into them.

The loud knocking came again, even faster and harder.

"Just a second!" he yelled.

He sat up in bed and rubbed his eyes a few times, then opened them again. It went better this time, and he was slowly able to take in his surroundings.

His head hurt like he had been hit the night before or

he had a hangover, but he was pretty sure neither of those applied.

No, if he remembered clearly from the previous night, it had been his intention to not even fall asleep.

Had he been derelict in his duties as a friend and nodded off anyway? He shook his head to clear it. That wasn't like him, and yet the evidence was to the contrary.

More knocking came, so fast and hard it threatened to shake the door apart. This time, it was accompanied by the sound of a man yelling at him.

Not just any man - that voice belonged to Gabriel.

Harvey had no idea what Gabe was doing out there at this hour of the morning.

Harvey groaned again and quickly scanned the room. Everything seemed to be in place. The room was nice and tidy, Sariah's clothes were folded neatly on her bed. Nothing out of the ordinary.

Then memories of the night before hit him like a ton of bricks. Sariah had slept in his room last night. But now she was nowhere to be found.

A knot of fear formed in his stomach and he shot up out of bed. Sariah was gone! He had to find her.

He moved over to the doorway and flung it open. On the other side, he saw Gabe looking scared and preparing to knock again. The man's face was ragged and it looked like he'd barely slept.

"Sariah's gone!" the two said to each other in unison.

"Wait, you know?" Gabe replied, cocking his head to the side.

"Yeah. She was with me last night, but now she's gone and disappeared."

Gabe's eyes grew wide and filled with anger. "You just slept through the whole thing?" He wagged a finger at the younger man. "What were you thinking, you dolt!"

Harvey reared back. "Now wait a second, it's not like that! I tried to stay awake all night just to help her." He looked critically at the older man. "Not like you were any help. You were the cause of her mood yesterday."

Gabe pointed a finger at himself. "Me?" Harvey nodded. "Nonsense," he said while shaking his head. "Utter nonsense!" The older man sighed. "Look, none of this is getting us anywhere. Sariah is out there somewhere by herself and we need to go find her."

"We can certainly agree on that," Harvey admitted. "Let me get my pack and we'll get going."

"That's more like it. Hurry up, we must leave as soon as we can if we're to catch up."

Harvey walked about his room and started throwing things into an oversized sack. He took anything he could think of, not sure just where they'd end up going or doing to get Sariah back.

A strange thought came to him then and he stopped what he was doing to look at Gabe. "Any idea where she might have gone?"

Gabe shook his head. "No, but Bear went with her. Wherever she is, she's in trouble."

Harvey's heart sank. That dog adored her. If Bear was gone, too, then it must be serious.

The older man tapped his arm and leveled his gaze at Harvey. "Time's a-wasting. Come on, let's hurry!"

"Psh," Harvey replied with a wave of his hand. "Believe

me, you don't need to convince me of the urgency on this one."

"Just hurry up! If we're quick, we might be able to catch her before she's able to leave town!"

Harvey narrowed his eyes and furrowed his brow. "What makes you so sure she's headed out of town?"

Gabe rolled his eyes. "Where else would she go?"

"I guess you have a point there." He gathered up the last few items and slung the pack over his shoulder. "Let's get going."

Sariah walked through the trees as fast as her feet would take her. She looked over her shoulder for signs that someone was following her for about the thousandth time that day, but there was no one there.

It had been four days since she'd left Harvey in Stratton. She was surprised both that no one had caught up to her, and that she'd gotten as far as she had. She moved a lot faster in general now, and it was easier to go somewhere by yourself than it was in a group. Especially when you barely stopped moving.

She knew the area pretty well by now, having traversed it a few times, and she knew exactly where she was headed, as did Bear.

She looked down at the dog and gave him an appreciative pat on his back. Bear looked up at her and gave her a quick bark.

That dog had been her truest companion for the past few days, always standing alert and finding her some of the best paths through the woods.

She thought about what Valerie had told her about Gabe killing Jakob and being an altogether bad man. She didn't know if she was putting too much faith in the old woman's words, coming out here like this on her own to find out for herself.

She should have given Gabe the benefit of the doubt. Sariah bit her lip. He'd never been mean to her in the past, and he certainly didn't seem like the killer type. Maybe she should just go back and apologize.

It was the same conversation she'd played in her head about a dozen times a day. Each time, it ended the same way. She shook her head to clear it. She'd come this far. It was time to finish what she'd started.

Gabe scowled for about the tenth time that day. He looked at Harvey, who was wearing one of his typical dopey grins and scowled again for good measure.

It was bad enough he was traveling alone with the kid. The only thing that made it worse was why they were traveling together in the first place.

His thoughts trailed to Sariah. *Where is that stupid girl?* he asked himself.

Summoning forth his magic power, he felt for her presence. It was something he did several times a day now, ever since they'd learned Sariah had somehow slipped out of Stratton in the middle of the night and had who knows how big of a lead on them.

It took a moment, but the answer came quickly enough.

She was south of them and heading even further south. She could be headed back home toward Chatwick. He supposed it made a certain amount of sense, but why?

Only one answer came to him. She knew the truth about his past and was running away from him. But why? Wasn't she different? Didn't she trust him? Not that he'd ever given her reason to.

For a moment, Gabe considered teleporting to her position. It was a risky move with Harvey in tow, especially when he wasn't sure where exactly he'd end up. They were gaining on her fast enough and would catch up soon.

"Are we gaining on her?" Harvey asked.

Gabe sighed and shook his head. It was only the fifth time that day he'd asked, and it was getting on his nerves.

"Not really," he told the kid.

"How do you even know where she is, anyway?"

Gabe rolled his eyes. "Magic, remember? Mental magic. It's how Sariah found you back when you were kidnapped. Same thing." Normally he couldn't track her, but she seemed to have let her guard down. Likely because she was flustered.

Harvey's eyes brightened. "Oh yeah! Okay then."

Gabe looked up at the sky. The clouds were darkening and it looked like it would start raining any second.

Just great, he thought. The last thing I need is more rain.

He didn't have long to focus on it. He'd found Sariah. She was not too far ahead, and she'd stopped moving.

Only she wasn't in Chatwick.

Sariah felt more than saw the little stream she'd crossed all those weeks ago in search of Gabe originally. Only way back then, she hadn't even known it was Gabe she'd been searching for. And, today, she still wasn't.

The young girl sighed and took in another deep breath. Gabe's cabin was not far ahead. She'd have the answers she sought soon enough, one way or another. She just had to keep pressing on.

Soon enough, the trees gave way and she was at the little cabin in the woods. It looked cold and dead inside, much like her she felt. Not warm and inviting like it had been when she'd first woken up inside it.

A sigh escaped her lips. How times change. Those days felt like they belonged to another lifetime entirely.

Bear, at her side, gave off a knowing bark and looked at her expectantly.

Sariah looked down at the animal. "We're here, Bear. You know what to do."

The dog looked at her once, nodded his head, and started moving around the clearing, pawing at various things as he went.

At the same moment, it started raining. Not a pleasant rain, either, but a harsh one. The droplets came down fast, splashing into the ground and making puddles in the cracked dirt.

She groaned and wiped at her eyes, then steeled herself. She was on a mission. A little rain wasn't going to stop her and might help. She had to finish this and find evidence of Gabe's misdeeds, or go back to him and apologize.

Her eyes scanned the ground. By all reports, Jakob had lived rather peacefully in this cabin for years. If he really were dead, there was a chance his body would be around here somewhere.

Gabe was strong, but he likely wouldn't have wanted to take the body far away even if he'd had the wherewithal to do it.

She looked at Bear. He was still pawing away at the ground at various spots. She wondered for a moment what he thought about all of this. The animal was betraying his master, in a way, and yet he seemed completely willing to do it.

What did that say about Gabe's character if he could befriend such a nice animal? Surely, he couldn't be all bad.

Sariah bit her lip and shook her head again. Such thoughts would do her no good. Finding the truth would. It's why she'd come out here. She put her head down and went back to searching for any mound or marker that could possibly be a gravesite.

She didn't have high hopes for finding anything. Why would Gabe have gone through the trouble of marking the grave of someone he'd killed? That wouldn't make any sense, and above all else when Gabe did things, they typically made sense, but it was all she had to go on.

A moment later, she heard Bear barking from the far side of the clearing. He was standing on top of a small mound of dirt, pawing at the ground frantically.

Sariah squinted to see what the animal was pawing at through the rain, but couldn't quite make it out.

"What is it, Bear?" she asked. The dog kept barking.

She walked over to him slowly, half-afraid of what she might find and not even sure she wanted to. She really wasn't sure anymore. It felt like a loss for her at this point.

She took another step forward and almost slipped in fresh mud. She put out a hand to steady herself and then took another step forward.

Sariah took in a deep breath to calm her nerves. That had been a close call. She'd almost fallen over in the mud and ruined whatever surprise Bear had for her.

Feeling a little better, she opened her eyes and took in the scene before her. Her stomach churned and her heart ached. Bear had found something, all right.

It was raining in earnest. Gabe looked up at the sky and groaned. The rain didn't suit his current mood.

He glanced at Harvey. The kid didn't even seem to be fazed by the stuff.

Gabe checked for Sariah with his magic again. She was at his old cabin, that much was certain. What on Irth could have led her there?

In his mind, he could only think of one reason and it wasn't good. This was not how he'd wanted her to find out. This could only end badly.

Had that stupid dress merchant known about me all along? he wondered.

A pit formed in the base of his stomach and he felt a little queasy. His teeth clenched. This was all that Valerie's fault. He would have to go back and do something about her when this was over.

First, he had to do something about the kid traveling with him. It wouldn't do for Harvey to find out about him like this. Besides, now more than ever, he wanted to confront Sariah alone.

Gabe sighed and shook his head. "I can feel Sariah," he told Harvey.

The kid's ears shot up. "Yeah?"

He nodded. "Yeah. She's right up ahead through the trees."

Harvey grinned at him. "What are you waiting for? Let's get going!"

The kid started to bolt forward through the trees. Gabe just sighed again. "Not so fast, kid."

He cast a magic spell to put the kid to sleep. It was a gentle enough spell, and it suited his purposes for the time being. The poor kid crumpled where he stood and fell onto the ground backward with a loud thud.

Gabe walked up and looked the kid over. Harvey's head looked a little bruised from the fall but other than that it looked like he'd be fine.

"Nighty-night, Harvey," he said with a long sigh. "It was fun while it lasted." Then he was off.

—————

Sariah looked down at the pile of bones and rotting flesh in shock and horror. There was no denying it, there was a dead body at her feet. If it hadn't been for the harsh rain, Bear likely never would have found it, but there it was.

It was hard to know for certain if it was Jakob's body. For one, she had no idea what the man had looked like. Second, even if she had, it would be hard to tell with the state of this corpse.

The rain started to die off and Sariah heard the sound of a twig breaking behind her. Her blood froze and she turned slowly, knowing all too well who she'd find there.

He was alone and looked a little worse for wear from the rain and the travel. There was a worried look in his eyes and he had his hands out in front of him.

"Hi Sariah," he said slowly. The words seemed to roll off his tongue.

She took half a step backward and said nothing.

Gabe took another step forward. She freaked and unsheathed her sword, holding it in front of her like a protective barrier.

"Easy now, Sariah," Gabe continued, holding his hands in front of him. "I can explain everything."

Blood shot up into Sariah's cheeks, setting them on fire. Her eyes burned with anger and passion. "Explain what?" she demanded. "How you've been lying to me this whole time, or how you're really a murderer?"

Gabe sighed and rolled his eyes. He glanced down at the remains of Jakob. "Oh," he said. "So you found his remains, then."

Sariah nodded slowly. "Yeah, I found them. And so much more besides."

He pulled on his face and took another half-step forward. "Look, it's not what you think."

"Stay back!" she yelled at him. She backed up another half step and thrust her blade forward.

"Come on, Sariah! This is me you're talking about. Let me explain."

"I don't want to hear more of your excuses!" she insisted, spitting on the ground in his direction. "You lied to me! You're still one of them! One of those people that murdered my parents! How can I forgive that?"

Gabe held up his hands in front of his face. "Please, Sariah, listen to reason. What if I'd told you the truth back then? Do you think you would have listened? I needed to wait until things calmed down, for your own protection."

"Until things calmed down? What, am I just some petulant little kid to you?" She flicked her sword about. "I said stay back!"

Gabe took a slight step back. "That's not what I meant, Sariah, and you know it. Look, yes, it's true. I killed Jakob, though in fairness he had it coming. And I am still with the Dusk Ravens. Well, sort of. Not with their main force, really."

He pulled on his face again. "You don't understand. The Master has a power unlike anything you could comprehend. It would be foolish to fight against him. The only safe place in the world is standing by his side."

Sariah scoffed. "No, you're the one that doesn't understand. I could never side with that monster. Not after what he did to my parents. And for what? Some stupid piece of jewelry?" She hung her head low. "How could you?"

Gabe took another step forward. "That was all just a misunderstanding. Please, come with me and I'm sure we can make him see the light."

He held out his hand to her and Sariah responded by lunging at him with her blade. Gabe dodged out of the way quickly to avoid getting impaled.

"See the light?" she replied incredulously. "Is that all you take me for?" She balked. "A mistake?"

Gabe rolled his eyes again. "It's not like that. Just please, give me a chance to make things right!"

Her stomach lurched and her heart sank even further. How could she have been so wrong?

She lowered her head. "Go away! Go away and leave me alone!"

Gabe sighed once more and shook his head. "You know I can't do that, Sariah. Not anymore. Please, don't make it end like this."

"Like what?" She stared at him and made more furtive motions with her sword. "Just stay back already!"

Gabe sighed one last time. "So be it." He pulled out his own sword and motioned for Sariah to come and attack him.

For a moment, she wanted to drop her blade and fall into his arms. To say she was sorry and tell him everything would be okay somehow. Desperately, she wanted to believe it could be.

Staring at Gabe's weapon drawn and facing her, she knew it never could be. There was only one path left open to her now. She clenched her teeth and tightened the grip on her blade.

A righteous anger filled her then as she looked at Gabe not as a friend or a teacher, but as an opponent.

She wasted no time, moving in with a thrust toward his midsection which was easily parried. She followed up with a few quick sideways strikes, all of which Gabe managed to bat away with ease.

Sariah screamed and made a hard lunge for his head. This blow, too, was knocked away. She made a few more attempts to hack him to pieces, but none of them were successful. She couldn't manage to hit him, but he wasn't fighting back, either.

His lack of offense incensed her further. "Fight me!" Sariah demanded. "Have I not earned that much respect from you, at least?"

Gabe shook his head and looked at her. There was pity in his eyes.

"Attack me!" she screamed. "Fight me like a man!" She came in with a low swipe toward his legs then, which he again batted away like a seasoned pro.

"As you wish," Gabe replied.

His blade finally moved, then, coming at her sword arm so fast she could barely see the blade move, let alone move her own weapon up to meet it.

The sword sliced into her arm, leaving a nasty cut. Pain shot up her arm and she dropped her blade. Another thrust came then, slicing across her stomach. She was defenseless to stop it.

Fortunately, the blade didn't sink in deep, but the pain was unimaginable. Sariah sank to her knees.

She looked up at Gabe, her eyes full of fire and fury. She managed to summon forth a fireball and she flung it up at him with all her might, but it never made an impact. Instead, she watched as it dissipated against Gabe's shield harmlessly.

Sariah screamed and fired forth more fireballs, but none of them connected. They just bounced off his shield like he wasn't even trying.

Gabe let his blade fall to his side and held up a hand in defense. "Enough," he said. "Please, just stop." He held out his hand to her. "Come on, put an end to this, and we'll talk. I'll be honest with you about everything and tell you whatever you want to know. I promise."

Sariah took a moment to steady her breathing and stared at the offered hand. For a brief moment, her anger faded, and she thought about taking it.

Maybe she was wrong. Maybe the other path was still open to her and she could go back to the way things had been several days ago. She'd been so happy then. Deliriously so. She longed for that safety and security once again for just a moment.

The moment passed and her face hardened again. That path was as dead as Gabe's old mentor.

With the last of her strength, she spit on Gabe's outstretched hand.

Gabe recoiled, his face contorted in equal parts shock and anger, and he scowled at her. "Fine!" he shouted. "Have it your way!" He summoned forth a fireball of his own.

Just then, Bear shot forward, placing himself between Sariah and Gabe. The dog growled and gnashed his teeth at Gabe.

The older man let the fireball drop. "Not you too, Bear?" he asked his dog.

Bear growled again and pawed at him until Gabe backed up a step.

Gabe shook his head. "Fine," he said again. "Have it your way." He looked at Sariah. "You can keep the damn dog. He always seemed to prefer you anyway."

Sariah smiled smugly, glad that she could at least get this one small victory, even if she couldn't best him in battle. It was a petty victory, but one that looked like it would save her from certain doom. At least for today.

"Go away!" Sariah spat at him.

Gabe rolled his eyes. "Grow up, Sariah," he spat back at her. Then he turned and left. Sariah could hear the sound of his footsteps moving away from her, then even that noise faded.

She was now well and truly alone.

Exhausted and in pain, Sariah collapsed onto the ground. She clutched at the wound in her stomach. Was it fatal? She didn't think so, but she had no way to know for sure. Out here on her own like this, it could end up that way.

She looked up at the sky. As if to spite her, the clouds were starting to give way once more to the sun. Even the sky seemed to have forsaken her in her hour of need.

Her attention turned to Bear. The dog was looking quite pleased with himself. He whined, then, and nuzzled the wound in her stomach.

"It's okay, Bear," Sariah lied. "It's all going to be just fine."

She closed her eyes and let the reality of her situation sink in. She was injured, could barely move, and the person she had fallen for had turned out to be her sworn enemy.

Not exactly her best day, all things considered.

Then she cried, long and hard. It was a long time before the tears stopped flowing.

CHAPTER SEVENTEEN

Sariah looked up at the sky, then over at Bear. The mutt was standing over her with a worried expression on his face.

Her stomach wound throbbed. She tried to move, but the pain kept her in place. It hurt even worse than before. That was probably her own fault, too. She'd managed to crawl out of the mud earlier, but it hadn't been fun, and it had only aggravated the wound more.

Turning her focus away from the wound, she noticed her lips were cracked and dry, which seemed odd to her since it had been raining pretty hard not a half-hour earlier.

It was probably from blood loss. She licked them once to try and make them feel better, but her tongue felt thick and heavy in her mouth and barely responded to her commands.

A sigh escaped her lips, then she admonished herself for the action. Sighing was Gabe's signature move, and she didn't want anything to do with him. Not right now, at least.

Worse, it made her lips feel even more cracked and dried than before.

Bear let out a low whine and looked at her with a tinge of sadness and pity in his eyes. He was a good animal for staying with her and betraying his master.

What had that cost him? she wondered. The decision must have been a hard one for him.

"I know, Bear," she muttered. "It doesn't look all that great right now, does it?"

The dog shook his head and gave her one quick bark.

Sariah let out a slight chuckle, which only made her lips and stomach hurt even worse, so she cut it off quickly.

"It'll get better soon, Bear," she told the dog. She reached out and patted his big, long head with one of her hands. The motion stung a little bit, but it was worth it to bring the dog some level of comfort.

Inwardly, she scoffed. She knew just how untrue those words were. She thought about the direness of her situation and about Gabe. Her mind's eye went back to the kiss they'd shared in Stratton, and she involuntarily brought a hand up to her lips and gingerly pressed it to them.

She could still feel that kiss there, and still felt a longing for him. It made her heart ache, and at the same time it made her want to puke.

Laughter came to her, unbidden. She shook her head and another jab of pain shot to her forehead in response. She really was in quite the predicament and didn't see any way out of it. She was too injured and tired to keep moving, and no one would find her all the way out here.

She looked at Bear one more time. The dog seemed to take notice of her dark train of thought and was whining at her and nudging her with his nose.

He really was a good dog. She gave him one more pat on his head and scratched behind one of his ears.

"It'll be okay, Bear," she lied again. "Everything will be just fine."

Harvey blinked a couple of times against the harshness of the sun beating down on him. His head hurt like he'd hit it on something, and his clothes were soaking wet.

That's odd, he thought. Why would I have taken a nap in a rainstorm?

He shook his head to try and clear it and the pain intensified. He reached behind his head with one hand and felt a nice, round bruise there at the base of his skull.

"Ugh," he said, rolling his eyes. "Why do things like this keep happening to me?"

There was no use worrying about it for too long. He decided to get up and look for Gabe. If he'd been knocked unconscious, maybe something bad had happened to him, too.

He got up on his knees and then pushed himself into a standing position. It was harder than it should have been like he was still weak and groggy from sleeping.

Looking at his surroundings, everything suddenly came flooding back. Sariah running off alone, upset and confused. He and Gabe chasing her through the woods back toward Chatwick.

Gabe had told him they were catching up to her, and then all of a sudden, he'd felt overly tired and everything had gone black.

His slight grin turned into a frown. He recognized that feeling from before. Gabe had put him to sleep using his magic. That bastard.

There was only one reason he could think of - so Gabe could face Sariah alone. Not that that reason made any sense to him, either. What could have possibly transpired to make Gabe want to face Sariah alone like that? Harvey didn't know what he had missed.

His hands formed into fists involuntarily and he had to force himself to unclench them and take a deep breath to calm his nerves. Anger wasn't going to help him. He needed calm, reasoned thought to guide his steps. Cooler heads always prevailed.

After a few moments, he'd calmed down enough to think clearly. He took a look around. The area looked vaguely familiar and he was pretty sure he'd been here before.

Then it hit him - these were the woods near Gabriel's old cabin. The very place they'd gone at the start of their grand adventure all those months ago. Sariah and Gabe must have been headed that way.

Harvey looked down at his side and saw his blade was still in its scabbard. The thought made him feel safer. He wasn't sure why he'd need it, but just in case it couldn't hurt.

With one hand on the hilt of his sword, he took a few furtive steps through the trees.

Vincent walked through the Alpenwood without a care in the world. It had rained recently, and he so loved walking the woods after a good rainstorm.

The water had such a remarkable effect on the undergrowth. The plants and trees sang their praises after a good, old fashioned rainstorm. There really was nothing quite like it.

He strolled along one of the old paths through the trees that only his people knew about and hummed softly to himself. It was an old tune, said to be formed before the dark days that had torn Irth apart. Of course, he had no way to know if that was really true, but he liked the thought of it.

He glanced down at his familiar Ferdinand. The red-tailed fox was flitting about and running in between his legs.

A smile crept across Vincent's lips. He could tell today was going to be a good day.

Just then, Ferdinand stopped and perked up his ears straining to hear something from far away.

Vincent's smile turned to a frown and he looked at the animal quizzically. "What is it, boy?" he asked.

The fox looked up at his master briefly, then went back to his previous pose.

Vincent knelt and gently stroked Ferdinand's back. "Come boy, what's wrong?" he tried again.

Ferdinand shook his head rapidly and went back to the same pose.

The druid sighed and rolled his eyes, then stood and

started walking again. "Come along, Ferdinand. Time's a-wasting and we're a way from our home still."

He looked back over his shoulder at the animal, but it didn't budge.

Something was definitely amiss. It could be hard to tell with Ferdinand sometimes. When he acted up like this, it could be anything from a person being in trouble to a squirrel ferreting up a tree.

Vincent walked back over to his familiar and pulled lightly on one of its paws. "Come now, boy. Let's get going."

Still the animal wouldn't budge. Instead, he flashed his fangs at Vincent and growled at him.

Vincent reared back. "Now, now, Ferdinand. That's no way to behave. Come on!" He pulled at the beast's front paw again, harder this time.

Ferdinand responded by snapping at his master's hand.

Vincent withdrew his hand quickly and thought about reprimanding his familiar further, but then he heard an odd noise.

It was coming from far away, so it was hard to make it out, but the forest was carrying the noise to him for a reason. He was sure of it. It sounded like an animal's whine.

Vincent's blood froze and he looked at Ferdinand with renewed respect. "Someone's in trouble, aren't they boy?" the druid said to his familiar.

Ferdinand nodded his head once.

The druid straightened up and stroked his beard a time or two. "Well, what are we waiting for? Let's get going."

Sariah looked up at the sun. It was hard to know if it had moved since she'd stared at it last. She thought maybe it had, but the days were long at this time of year and it was impossible to know.

A bead of sweat formed on her brow and dripped into her eye. It stung and she wiped it away with her free hand. Every inch of her seemed to protest the motion and a fresh wave of pain rocked through her core.

She let out a yelp of pain. Even that seemed to hurt. She marveled that responding to her pain caused her even more pain. It was like her body was playing a dark, twisted game with her, one she couldn't possibly win.

Just my luck, she thought grimly.

She could do little else but wait it out. It was impossible there'd be anyone out there waiting to come to save her. Her situation was hopeless.

"At least you'll live to tell my tale," she told Bear.

He let out another long, low whine and she patted him on the head again. The animal let his head rest on her chest. His warmth was somehow comforting to her, so she didn't argue.

She tried to crane her head to take a look at her stomach wound, but Bear's massive furry head blocked it fully from view.

A smile formed on her cracked lips. He was a constant companion, even here at the end.

Sariah raised her hand that had been holding her stomach wound and looked at it. The blood on it looked dry and flaking, not fresh and wet like before. She didn't know if that was a good sign or a bad one. She let the hand fall back onto her middle.

The coughing started then, each one racking her body and filling her abdomen with fresh waves of pain.

She returned her focus to Bear and noticed her eyes were getting blurry and the animal was hard to make out, even though he was only a few inches from her face.

Is this what the end feels like? she wondered, and let out a stifled laugh. *How would I know, anyway?*

It was a fair question. It wasn't like you could go up to someone and ask them what it felt like moments before death. Anyone who'd experienced it was going to be a little hard to reach.

She laughed again, then, and coughed straight afterward. Then she let out one last cry of pain because the combined action hurt like hell. It seemed her body wasn't quite ready to let her out of this hell just yet.

Her eyes closed as a chill sensation washed over her and the pain somehow lessened. A little at first, and then quite a bit all at once.

With a slight grin on her face, everything went black.

***

Harvey crept forward through the trees, wondering what he was going to do once he finally came face to face with Gabe and Sariah. He didn't know what he was going to say to them exactly.

It was pretty obvious they'd wanted privacy, but he was too worried about her to care. A feeling in his gut that wouldn't let go told him something was gravely wrong. What, he couldn't be sure, but it was something big.

He heard a shrill cry break through the stillness of the trees up ahead.

The hair on the back of his neck stood on edge and he froze. That was Sariah's voice and she was in pain!

Harvey tightened his grip on his sword and pulled it free from its sheath. There was no telling what was waiting for him, only that Sariah needed him and this time, he was going to be there for her.

He bounded through the trees as fast as his feet could carry him, barely paying attention to the ground. Ordinarily, that would be a risky maneuver in the deep woods, but he didn't care, and thankfully he didn't trip on anything as he sped on.

Another cry came then, weaker but closer to where he was. His chest tightened and his heart skipped a beat.

He thought about answering her cries with one of his own, but that could announce his presence to whoever was still there, and prove deadly if it was an enemy. Better to have the element of surprise.

He kept going, moving swiftly and quietly through the trees toward Gabe's cabin. He was only a few meters away from the clearing.

When he finally broke through the trees, he beheld quite the sight. Sariah was on the ground not far away from him, and there was a strange man kneeling over her. Gabe was nowhere to be seen.

Harvey brought his weapon up. "Get off her!" he cried, waving his blade toward the imposing stranger.

When the man didn't budge, he took another step

closer and summoned forth a fireball, readying it to fly into the stranger's face.

"I said get off her!" he repeated. Still, the man didn't budge.

Harvey took another step and pulled his hand back to let loose the fireball when he caught a slight glimpse of something red and furry in his peripheral vision.

He blinked and then turned his attention to this new threat. It was none other than Ferdinand, and he seemed to be nipping at Bear's paws, trying to get the dog's attention.

The young warrior took another look at the man kneeling over Sariah. He recognized the man's face, then. It was Vincent, the kind druid who had helped him in the Battle of Chatwick.

His neck muscles and the tension in his hands loosened a half step and he let the fireball drop. Vincent wouldn't harm Sariah. He was sure of that. The man was far too gentle to do anything of the sort. Besides, he and Sariah had helped him earlier.

He took another couple of steps to close the distance between them and looked at Vincent, then took a good, hard look at Sariah.

What he saw brought a tear to his eyes. She looked unconscious, which was good considering the rest of her. There was a pretty hefty cut in her arm and her stomach was torn open. There was dirt and blood covering her entire lower half. Whatever had happened, it hadn't been good.

Harvey looked up from Sariah's tattered form and at Vincent. The druid's eyes were glowing a fierce green and he was gently holding Sariah's broken body in his own hands, focusing intently.

It didn't take much for Harvey to figure out what was going on. The druid was doing his best to heal her.

He took a step back and let the older man continue his work, thankful for his presence. Sariah's wounds were pretty heavy. He was fairly certain he wouldn't have been able to handle them with just bandages.

Speaking of healers, though, where is Gabe? he wondered. Why did he let her get injured like this? Unless...

A dark thought came to him, then, and suddenly it all made sense. Gabe had been the one to cause those injuries. Sariah had fought with him. But why?

He shook his head. He'd ask Sariah about it later.

Vincent blinked and raised his head. He smiled as he caught sight of Harvey. "Is that you, Harvey?" Vincent asked.

He nodded. "In the flesh."

Vincent's smile grew broader. "I'm glad you're here." He looked down at Sariah then back up at Harvey. He pushed her body forward a little bit. "This is for you," he said like he was offering Harvey a present.

Harvey chuckled and took Sariah's body. She felt lighter than normal somehow, though looking over her, it looked whole again. Filthy, but whole.

"Thank you," Harvey replied. "How did you find her? And what happened?"

The druid lowered his head. "Ferdinand led me here, but as to what happened, that I do not know."

"Well thank you, anyway." He looked down at Sariah again. She looked peaceful laying in his arms.

Harvey returned his gaze to Vincent. "Will she wake soon?"

The older man shook his head. "It's hard to know for certain. Her body I can heal, but her soul, that is a different matter." Vincent's eyes darkened and his face hardened. "Something terrible happened here today. Of that, I can be sure. What exactly it was is hard to know, but it affected your friend here deeply."

Harvey thought he knew what it was, and he didn't like it one bit. He nodded at the older man. "I'll take care of her. No matter how long it takes."

Vincent smiled at him and placed a hand on his shoulder. "I know you will, lad." He got up, then, and shook his legs a time or two, stumbling in the process.

Harvey started to get up to help him, but Vincent waved him off. "I'm all right, lad. A little weary from the healing is all, but I'll recover." The druid looked at Sariah once more. "Take care, you two."

Then the older man turned and left. He whistled once, and Ferdinand stopped playing with Bear and followed after.

Within a few moments, Harvey, Bear, and Sariah were alone. He looked down at his friend. She looked so peaceful in her unconscious state.

He reached around pulled her to him and embraced her for a moment, hoping it would wake her up, but nothing happened.

"You're safe now, Sariah," he told her. "Safe and sound."

Harvey's mind drifted. There were a lot of dangers still

lurking out there for the two of them. The Dusk Ravens. The Master. And now Gabe was seemingly against them, too.

They had many trials still to face for sure, but for right now, the danger had passed and the two of them were okay. They could face the rest of their trials tomorrow.

Today they were at peace. Today, they could rest.

She'd trusted her mentor. How could she have been such a fool?

Wounded and betrayed, Sariah now has two monsters to stop. Will she prevail before her friends are killed? Find out in Survival by Magic!

THE STORY CONTINUES

Wounded and betrayed, Sariah now has two monsters to stop. Will she prevail before her friends are killed?

Find out in Survival by Magic*!*

Grab your copy today at Amazon and Kindle Unlimited.

AUTHOR NOTES - PETER GLENN
JULY 17, 2020

First of all, thank you so much for reading through this entire book, and for now reading these author notes! It means the world to me to be able to share these characters and this journey with you! If it weren't for you fans, I would never have become an author.

What a ride, huh? I really enjoyed working on this book, and probably spent more time writing and re-writing it than I did any of the other Sariah Chronicles novels. This was a very important book to get right as it shows Sariah finally starting to really come into her own.

And of course the whole betrayal bit by Gabriel was something else. That was a scene that I had to get exactly right. I probably re-wrote that scene three or four times, fine-tuning it each time. I'd known from the start that Gabe was going to betray her, but not how. Watching it all unfold as I typed it out was a very rewarding experience (in a strange way, I mean, he *was* betraying her after all, but it was still fun to get right).

How about you? What was your favorite scene in

Betrayal of Magic? I'd love to know. Drop me a line at peter@peterjglenn.com and let me know! I absolutely love hearing from my fans, and respond to each and every one of you individually. There's nothing better for me as an author than to hear from my fans.

Anyway, believe it or not, I wrote the majority of this book over a long three day weekend. I was holed up in a hotel for a business trip and had lots of time on my hands so I figured, why not write as much of this book as I could.

It was like a little challenge or contest that I had with myself to see if I could beat my daily or weekly word count records.

The end result? I wrote 40,000 words over three days. That beat my all-time weekly record handily, but believe it or not, it didn't beat my daily record. Nope, that was set way back when I was 18 and freshly out of high school. It was the summer between high school and college, and I was working on my original trilogy (don't worry, you'll hear more about that in the near future, it's coming out in the later part of 2020).

I had a lot of time on my hands during those days. Too much, even, since I didn't have homework or a job. So I spent a lot of it writing. And on one such day, I managed to eke out 20,000 words in one go. That's still my record, and I'm not sure I'll ever beat it. At least not while I have children under 2 in the house. I love my little bundles of joy, I do, but they're not conducive to long writing stretches.

And with the pandemic shutdown, the amount of time I have to devote to writing has only decreased. I used to escape the house every time I wanted to write something, but the options for leaving the home when everything around you is shut down are fairly minimal. So I'm learning to write through the distractions of a home life. It's slow going, but I have so many stories I want to share with you all that I wouldn't have it any other way.

Well, I had tons of fun writing this book, and I'm hoping you had a great time reading both the book and these notes. This here is my chance to give you a behind the scenes look at my processes and how my worlds develop, and I cherish every moment of it.

If you liked this book, *please* leave a review. It means the world to me. Each and every review is like a cherished treasure or a well-loved family heirloom. They're why I write (well that and to get paid, of course, but mostly it's to make readers like you happy).

Plus, a bunch of good reviews *might* just help that next book come out that much faster. There's still loads of adventures for Sariah left in my head just waiting to get put down on paper. Not to mention all the other characters that want their turn in the spotlight!

Loved the book a lot? Give me a follow on social media: www.facebook.com/authorpeterglenn OR join my mailing list: www.peterjglenn.com/email. Or heck, do both! The more the merrier!

I'd love to get a shout out from you in either spot and hear about what you'd like to see in an upcoming Sariah Chronicles adventure. Who knows? Maybe I'll even name a future character after you (if you ask nicely, of course).

Thank you again for joining me on this journey and sticking with it until the very end, and I do hope you'll join with me again in future books.

Auf Wiedersehen.

AUTHOR NOTES - MICHAEL ANDERLE
JULY 18, 2020

Thank you for reading our books and allowing us a chance to do what we love.

Create stories!

As I become an "old man" in this industry (I put air quotes around that because I'm not even five years old yet in this industry. I have a way to go yet. On the other side of that coin, I've been involved in hundreds of stories being published, so I've done a lot in a compressed time.)

Anyway, as a publishing five-year-old, I look back at the challenges when writing, and it seems like you have the perfect storm to confound your writing...

Every week.

It might not be children, but it could be an unexpected job, sickness, a friend coming into town, a holiday you forgot about ("Really, Thanksgiving is here so soon?") Similar to Peter, I've done (for me almost but not quite) 20,000 words in a day.

Unlike Peter, I NEVER intend to do that again if I can help it.

That effort taxed me enough that my body wants to shrink in terror at how much mental toil it took to make that happen. I have a hearty "Good-on-ya!" for Peter for 40,000 words in a weekend and the desire to do 20,000 again sometime in the future.

May he find the time with his children to write and cherish their memories. For myself, I didn't start really writing until our kids were juniors or so in high school and they weren't very needy with their time.

They had friends. Therefore I had time.

Now, all of our kids are out of the house, living their lives in another state. It's a weird part of my life with no children. Not better, not worse, but certainly quieter. I worry often, but there is nothing to be done about it.

Why didn't anyone bother telling me that AFTER they left the house, it wasn't over?

Like the characters in our books, our children have minds (and opinions) of their own. Whether they are two and throwing a fit when they don't like our no or twenty and just don't tell us what they are doing, both children and characters often go their own ways.

Keep going, Peter. Parenting both your children and your characters is a fulfilling career. I'm waiting for when my characters start asking for Christmas presents.

Enjoy life, folks!

Ad Aeternitatem,

Michael Anderle

OTHER BOOKS FROM LMBPN PUBLISHING

For a complete list of books from LMBPN Publishing please click the link below:

https://lmbpn.com/books-by-lmbpn-publishing/

CONNECT WITH THE AUTHORS

Peter Glenn Social

Website: www.peterjglenn.com

Email list: www.peterjglenn.com/email

Facebook:
www.facebook.com/authorpeterglenn

Michael Anderle Social

Website: http://lmbpn.com

Email List: http://lmbpn.com/email/

Facebook:
https://www.facebook.com/LMBPNPublishing